SYLVIA G. L. DANNETT and EDWIN BENNETT

DEFY THE TEMPEST

WILDSIDE PRESS

Chapter I

THE RAIN was beating savagely against the train windows, and through the streaming panes I could just make out the outline of naked trees being swept along by a great gale. To blot out the ominous sight, I looked again at the letter which I had received only a few days before.

I had read and reread it, and now I turned to it again.

"You have," I read, "been recommended by the Blakewell Agency and your credentials seem satisfactory."

When you have been out of a job for a long time, you are not offended by so trivial a thing as "seem," for any letter saying that you have at last found a job is good to look at.

Teaching positions were few then, especially after the fall semester had started, so this blunt letter brought a double happiness with it. If only everything turned out well, I would be able to earn enough money for Cousin Julian's much-needed operation. I even saw myself in that new spring outfit which I so badly needed. Of course, it seemed a little silly to think of spring with the approach of the new year only a matter of hours.

A long, drawn-out groan from the locomotive abruptly concluded my dreaming. I rubbed a small space clear on the glistening windowpane and peered out. It was dark now, but I could see a little depot lighted by one small lamp. All at once I was lonely, depressed. With a shriek, the train jolted into the darkness. The dreary little station was left behind, but my depression was not. I wanted to go right back to Julian's where I knew people who loved me, where I would not be so alone. A long time later the train stopped. I heard the conductor drone, "Seacliffe . . . Seacliffe." My train journey to the New England coast had ended. I had arrived.

I reached for my belongings which I had packed into three large bags. Taking one of the bags to the door, I returned to get the other two. Silently the conductor helped me take them off, and as quickly as he could, he jumped back into the train. In a moment it had roared into the streaming night.

I scanned the depot for some sign of life. But I saw no one. I hastily dragged my bags under the shelter of the depot's roof and tried its single door. It was locked. I sat down upon my bags. There seemed nothing else to do.

After a time I decided to brave the storm and the night and see where the road which circled the depot led. I was rounding the station building when suddenly twin beams of light flickered on the road and fell full upon me. I called out frantically. The driver of that car had to hear me. With a screech of its brakes it stopped. A man's voice rang out, "What's the matter?" And then more hopefully, "Want a taxi?"

"Oh, yes!"

He got out of the car and came toward me—a long, lanky individual.

"It bein' such a night, thought I'd better run over to see if there was anybody needin' a lift. Never can tell." He spoke with a slight drawl.

Happily I led him to my bags. He picked up two and I, carrying the other, ran to the auto. He started the car, and with a jolt we were off.

"Where you heading?" he asked, turning his head so he could get a good look at me.

"Meredith Hall. How far is it?"

"About three miles, all upgrade. Cost you a half piece." And then as if he thought his customer might want to come back, he added, "Seventy-five if you return."

That seemed reasonable enough. I lay back in the jolting car and listened to the storm's fury. The driver looked around at me again and said, "What you doing going to the Hall on New Year's Eve? Not throwing a party on top the hill, are they?"

"No, it isn't a party."

"Knew it wouldn't be. They never did throw any good parties there. And now especially there won't be any for a long time."

"Why not?"

"Somebody died there just before the Christmas holiday—one of the teachers. Everyone at the school is all broken up about it. Even Mrs. Hawkins."

"Who is Mrs. Hawkins?"

"House mother. 'Spect she'll be the only one home now. Miss Evangeline and Miss Helena and the rest of them went away over the vacation. First time for Miss Evangeline—wanted to get away from the death, I suppose. I take Mrs. Hawkins shopping once in a while—when the school bus is laid up for repairs."

"Who was the one that died?" I asked.

"Miss Vaughn—Eleanor Vaughn. She taught some highfalutin thing called art or something."

I gasped. He turned around again.

"What's the matter, cold?"

"No, I'm all right."

I could not explain to him the strange feeling which had swept over me when I realized that it was a dead person's place I was taking. The desolation I had felt in the train and on the depot platform surged up again. And I did not even have the dubious comfort of further talk, for just then the car's engine started to make a peculiar choking noise. Then it began to miss badly. A few terrifying chugs, and it stopped dead.

"Old Penelope's given up again," he said almost affectionately.

He got out and raised the hood of the engine but quickly put it down again as the rain splattered the hot metal and saturated the wires.

"No use," he said, getting into the car again. "It just won't go. Probably a wire's shorted, too."

"But what am I going to do?"

"Don't know. You can take my coat and go on up to the school. Isn't so far. Only 'bout half mile right along this road. You can't miss the gate. I'll walk as far as the highway, then try hitching to the village. Don't know how long I'll be. Too cold to stay in the car. I might not come back till morning." Then, as if it were an afterthought, he said, "Want me to go with you?"

"Not unless you want to," I said with spirit born of rage rather than courage, "but what about my bags?"

"I'll bring them up in the morning—Oh, you can trust me. I'm Jeggy Williams—deputy sheriff—" He touched a badge pinned to his vest. "Everybody knows me in the village. Lived here all my life. By the way, what's your name—you have my coat?"

"Hunter. Nancy Hunter."

I threw Jeggy Williams' coat around my shoulders, climbed out of the car, shouted good-by, and stumbled up the roadway.

I must have lost the main road, for I found myself on a wide, pebbled path. The stones were slippery and once I fell and bruised my knee. My hat was caught by a gust of wind and sailed into the night. I could not see in any direction. I stumbled and fell again. This time my hand felt rough wood beneath it. I picked myself up and rushed up what seemed low porch steps. I thought I saw a light glimmering inside the small building and I knocked loudly upon the door. I knocked again, but there was still no answer. I turned the doorknob and the door opened. Gratefully I went into the house.

"Anybody home?" I called.

The darkness seemed to muffle my voice. Remembering that there were some matches in my pocketbook, I took one out and struck it. In the flickering flamelight, I saw a lamp standing on a table. I fumbled for the cord, and for a moment the sudden brilliance blinded me. Then I saw something on a table. It was an umbrella, a green plaid umbrella. I touched it and found it to be wet. I had been right about the light.

"Hello," I called out.

But no one answered. I looked at the wet umbrella, and I was frightened. Obviously someone was here or had just been here. Why had that person not responded to my knock? Swiftly I looked about. I was standing in a hallway. Two doors led from this passageway— one on each side. I stepped cautiously into the doorway on the left. I felt along the wall near the door and found a switch. I snapped it on. I was in a large studio-like chamber and there were worktables and easels.

Two huge fireplaces jutted out between tall windows on the north and south sides, and on the east side was a very large opening—a great glassed-in arch. Plenty of good light in this room, the artist in me observed automatically. Then, hopefully, I went to one of the fireplaces intending to light a fire, but there was no kindling. The other fireplace was also swept clean. I moved to the large desk. Here I would doubtlessly be sitting for many class hours to come. I dropped down wearily, tired, cold, baffled.

The house groaned and creaked as the storm pounded it. Intermittently I heard the sea thundering and crashing, and always a single shutter clattering. I looked about the room again. Suddenly I gasped. But it was only a portrait, a half-finished canvas of a woman standing with the sea behind her. Neither the background nor the figure were formed in a definite shape, but the artist had already worked in the woman's face and had caught a startling expression in the eyes. They seemed to glare at me with hatred.

Crossing the hall, I entered the other room. It was twin to the one which I had just left, and the two fireplaces in this west wing were as empty as the ones in the east wing. A large double door appeared to be an entrance to a closet. The windows were tightly sealed, and a musty smell filled the room.

A clock chimed lingering notes. Better try getting to the school or it will be too late to find anyone to let you in, it reminded me. I carefully turned out the light and returned to the hall. I was about to go out into the storm again, when I thought of that wet umbrella. It was not on the table. Perhaps there had been no umbrella. Perhaps I had imagined it. I looked again. There were damp marks on the table where I had seen the umbrella, but it had vanished. I was puzzled—frightened.

I retraced my steps along the pebbled path until I reached the roadway, then started climbing the hill before me. Coming around a bend in the drive, I was confronted by a huge black structure. It stood out against the stormy night, and even in the darkness I could see that it resembled a medieval castle fashioned of wood and stone and crowned with impressive turrets. This was surely the main school building.

The gigantic entrance door loomed before me. I ran up the long flight of stone steps to it and rang the bell. Finally, a tall, thickset woman in a heavy nightgown and wrapper answered, held a lamp to my face. "Well?" she demanded.

"Please let me in," I cried. "I'm Nancy Hunter. I'm to teach here."

I stumbled through the doorway and slumped gratefully into a chair. The woman pushed the door shut and barred it. Then she turned on the hall lights, and just stared at me. She was a strange-looking female. Her high forehead was topped by a tangled mass of wispy gray hair, and her lower jaw sagged beneath an eagle-like nose.

"I'm Nancy Hunter," I explained again. "I'm to be the new art teacher. Miss Meredith sent for me."

She remained silent, waiting for me to continue.

"I came on early. The car broke down—Jeggy Williams' car."

"Where are your credentials?"

I opened my pocketbook and brought out the letter. "This is from Miss Evangeline Meredith."

"It's Miss Evangeline's signature," she grudgingly said. She looked at me sharply. "Why did you come before tomorrow? All the other teachers are away."

Briefly I explained why I had decided to come on to Seacliffe, but instead of mentioning finances, I stressed the idea that I was anxious to acquaint myself with the school before the students returned.

"And now if you please," I finished, "may I be shown my room? I'm tired and cold."

"Follow me," she said.

She turned the hall lights out and, holding the lamp high, she led the way up a long circular staircase. There were two of these staircases, one on either side of the hall, I noted automatically. We moved into a large hall from which three wings branched. Mrs. Hawkins, for I was sure that this was she, took the widest corridor which led through the main building. She stopped before a door halfway down the passage.

"This is to be your room," she said with an odd satisfaction.

We entered, and she switched on a small floor lamp.

"Change your things," she commanded. "You'll find something to wear in the closet."

She marched out of the room.

"Wait," I cried. "Is there—could I get something to eat? I haven't eaten anything since I left the city. I'll gladly pay—"

"You may have some tea, I suppose. I'll leave the back stairs lighted so you can see your way down. But don't be long. Bring your wet clothes with you. They will dry faster in the kitchen."

She vanished into the blackness of the great hall.

I stared about the room, my room. It was large, really stately. A bed supported on massive pillars of mahogany and hung with curtains of deep red damask stood like some fantastic Chinese temple in the center. Two large windows, with their blinds drawn, were half shrouded in festoons and falls of similar drapery. But for all its crimson richness, the room was cold, and I felt out of place in it.

I moved slowly about the room. I looked at a dressing table. Someone's very personal belongings were everywhere upon it. I looked at the splendid array of powder boxes and strangely shaped perfume bottles. They were extremely expensive and stood about as though someone had just left them and gone away.

"This won't do," I said airily. "I'm entitled to half the space."

I went to the wardrobe hoping to find some dry clothes to put on. I opened it and found a rack of good-looking clothes. I pulled out a comfortable blue chenille robe, slipped into it, gathered up my wet things, and following the back stair lights, descended to the kitchen. Mrs. Hawkins stood at the stove preparing tea, just what I wanted most.

"It will be ready in a moment. Lay your things on the chair by the stove." she spoke rather gruffly.

When I was sipping the hot tea, I asked Mrs. Hawkins who it was that was sharing my room with me.

"You are by yourself," she said.

"Then to whom do the things in my room belong?"

"They belonged to someone else. Someone who is now dead."

"Dead!"

Jeggy Williams' conversation flashed through my mind, and I realized immediately whose room I was occupying. I looked down at the dressing gown. There, lost in one of its rich, blue folds, were the initials *E. V.*

"But why were they left there? I don't want them in my room."

"Miss Evangeline wishes them to remain there until she returns. We did not know that you were coming while all the others were away."

"Couldn't I sleep in another room?"

"All the other bedrooms are locked. And the keys are with their owners. The girls' dormitory reeks with paint."

"Then we are the only ones here?"

"Yes, but Miss Evangeline and Miss Helena are expected back tomorrow. The servants will report in the morning."

I looked about at the immense kitchen.

"This is a very large place. . . . Certainly enough space to prepare food here."

"Oh, yes," a note of pride crept into her voice, "although this house was built almost a hundred years ago, it has been modernized to a great degree. The students study cooking here and use the new kitchen implements. The first Silas Meredith built this hall on the style of a medieval castle." She nodded her head in the direction of a kitchen closet. "He built that as a threat to his beautiful wife whom he didn't trust. You see, the door locks on the outside. Anyone trapped in there for more than a few hours would be suffocated."

I put my cup down abruptly.

"We'd better go to bed; it's past ten-thirty," she said.

"Oh, Mrs. Hawkins," I hoped my voice was gay, "ten-thirty isn't late for New Year's Eve."

She frowned at me and said sternly, "Ten o'clock is curfew time here, Miss Hunter. Miss Evangeline does not permit late hours or tolerate any frivolity on the part of the faculty. Especially now, while the entire school is under the death pall of one of whom we were all very fond."

"I'm sorry," I apologized.

When I was back in my room I locked the door. Hastily, I prepared for bed, wondering all the time if the sound of slamming shutters would ever stop long enough to permit sleep. My knee, although not bruised as much as I had anticipated, now pained dreadfully. The chill remained in the room, and I shivered again as I donned a nightgown and then the heavy blue chenille robe initialed *E. V.* What if its owner were dead and what if she had lived in this room and I was about to sleep in the very bed in which she had slept. I was alive. She was dead. That was life.

I crawled painfully into the big bed, all decided to shut my eyes and fall asleep immediately. I put my hand out to turn off the bedside lamp when suddenly I sat bolt upright and screamed. A face floated in the gloom opposite me, a woman's face. The lamp fell with a crash. I stopped screaming. The floating head was only a portrait. But what a portrait! The woman looked alive. Her eyes stared straight into mine. I jumped from the bed; the eyes followed me. I moved toward them. The face was handsome in a sharp sort of way. The small piece of metal fastened to the frame announced, "Emmeline Meredith."

I stood upon a chair and managed to turn the face to the wall. Then I went back to bed, switched off the light and almost immediately fell into a heavy, fitful sleep.

Chapter II

AT EIGHT o'clock I awoke, but sleep had not refreshed me. I ached all over, and I felt no inclination to get out of bed and begin my new life.

I lay there in that monstrosity of a bed, thinking about the mysterious E.V.

I climbed out of bed and promptly tripped over E.V.'s blue chenille robe which trailed about me. I was suddenly struck by the fact that it might have been designed for me, so well did it fit. It told me something about E.V. In stature she must have been of medium height, her form somewhat slender—like mine. This realization did not comfort me. I wandered restlessly about the room, trying to adjust myself to my new surroundings. An antique lover would have delighted in the magnificent furniture, but I longed for my more cheerful and utterly commonplace maple bedroom at home. A heavily carved mahogany desk suggested that I write to my Aunt Jennifer. Perhaps that would make me feel better. The desk was closed, but a handsome gold key hung in the lock. I fingered the key. Perhaps this desk would tell me more about E.V. I turned the key slowly and lowered the top.

Inside the desk a pale blue handkerchief with a lipstick smudge lay carelessly where it had been tossed into a corner. A nail file rested on the empty inkstand, and a white enameled cigarette case protruded from a tiny drawer. Something bright winked at me from the darkness of a cubbyhole. I picked up a single earring. It was a delicate hoop made of small diamonds and rubies. It was so alive that it seemed still warm.

The cubbyholes were filled with letters. Eleanor Vaughn must have had many friends. I had never had time to make many, I thought enviously. There had always been too much to do around the house. My spare hours had generally been spent with my cousin, Julian, and my few teaching assignments had been in small communities where there were few girls of my own age.

I stared at the letters fascinated. Who would know if I read one? I pulled out a batch of envelopes. They were from foreign countries, all addressed to Miss Eleanor Vaughn, care of Meredith Hall. Then, suddenly, I thrust them back into the desk. What right had I to delve into the private affairs of another woman, even though she were dead?

As I was about to shut the desk, a heavily scented sheet of paper slipped from beneath the soiled blotter. Written under the school letterhead was a brief salutation: "Dear Evelyn . . ." That was the only thing inscribed on the paper, but I was sure that this flowing salutation had been written by Eleanor Vaughn. Was it then "dear Evelyn" who had written those letters from abroad? I carefully closed the desk, turned the key in the lock and decided to stop this prying and imagining. Just then someone knocked on the door.

I went to the door, unlocked it, and flung it open. There was a gasp, and two objects struck the floor. I found myself looking into the frightened face of a servant girl.

"Sorry, Miss," she apologized, as she stooped to pick up my shoes which had slipped from her hands. "For a moment I thought . . . she had red hair, too."

"Who?"

"Miss Vaughn."

This was startling enough . . . I thanked her for bringing my clothes.

"That's all right, Miss. It's nice to have a young person like yourself to look after. I'm in charge of the faculty rooms." This last was uttered with an air of pride.

This girl could be a friend, I felt. I think she must have felt the same way, for she stayed to help me into my clothes although I had not asked her to do so.

"My name is Mary," she told me as she hooked the side of my skirt. "If there's anything you'll be needing I'll get it for you."

"Oh, thank you, Mary." It was good to hear this friendly, young voice. "I wonder," I continued, "if you would be good enough to remove Miss Vaughn's clothes. My own things will be arriving today, and—" I never finished the sentence, for Mary was obviously trembling.

"Please, Miss Hunter, it's Mrs. Hawkins you'll have to tell about that."

"Where can I find Mrs. Hawkins?"

"She's downstairs now." And suddenly, "Oh, Miss Hunter, I hope you'll be happy here with us."

"Why shouldn't I be happy here?"

"I'll be preparin' your breakfast, Miss," Mary said, ignoring my outburst.

At the door, she suddenly clasped her hand to her mouth and cried, "I almost forgot! Miss Evangeline would like to see you after you've eaten."

This news temporarily scattered all other thoughts. I was pleased now that I had come ahead of the others. Feeling lighter-hearted, I took a brief look in the mirror to make sure that my employer would find me satisfactory. I critically scrutinized the pair of green-gray eyes set a trifle too far apart, and put a light dab of powder on my thin, straight nose. A touch of lip rouge, and I was ready to face Miss Evangeline. I slipped quietly into the hall, and walked through the dimly lighted passage, my feet moving soundlessly across the heavy maroon carpeting. On the landing I hesitated.

I stood there recalling the little I knew about this family. They had made their mark in the field of education while steadily increasing their wealth. It was queer to think of having so much money bound up with a boarding school for girls. I vaguely remembered what Aunt Jennifer had said about the peculiar nature of one of the Meredith wills. It had something to do with Evangeline, but I wasn't quite sure what it was. It was a sordid affair according to Aunt Jennifer, and gave the family a good deal of unwholesome notoriety. Finally, the whole thing had been hushed up, and Evangeline Meredith had never again appeared in the news. I hurried down the circular flight of stairs, my shoulders squared, my chin up.

The entrance hall was deserted, but its magnificence was overwhelming. Marble pillars rose loftily from the marble floor to a gilded ceiling from which hung an enormous crystal and gold chandelier. On either side of the entryway was a closed door, with a name plate in the center panel of each. I paused in front of the first and read, *Philip James*. I crossed to the other door. This one bore the Headmistress' name.

I reached out to grasp a ponderous brass knocker when a woman's voice stopped me.

"Miss Hunter!" It was Mrs. Hawkins. "Miss Hunter, your breakfast is ready. Come this way."

She led me down a hall which ran straight to the rear, separating the rooms on either side of it. On the way, just where the passage was crossed by another corridor running the width of the building, I heard the sound of organ music.

"Who plays so beautifully?" I asked.

"Miss Evangeline. She is a great musician."

We entered the dining hall. This was surely the most unattractive, somber room in the building. Dingy gray walls were lined with pictures of a devout, biblical character.

Highbacked, heavily carved black chairs stood around the long black tables like pallbearers before a funeral casket. There were twelve tables, bare save for sugar bowls, salt and pepper shakers. Only a single place was set, at the far corner of the room, beside the thickly curtained windows. That was, I supposed, for me.

"Oh, Mrs. Hawkins," I said, as the housekeeper was leaving. "My things are coming this morning, and there is no place for them. Perhaps it would be possible to transfer me to another room today?"

"Miss Vaughn was satisfied with those quarters, Miss Hunter, but of course if you have any fault to find you had better take the matter up with Miss Evangeline."

I assured her that I was not trying to find fault with anything.

"I told you last night that I am only carrying out my orders," she said.

With that, she left the room.

Mary appeared with a pot of steaming coffee and a rack of crisp toast. She eyed me stonily, saying nothing as she set the remainder of my breakfast on the table. And without a word she returned to the kitchen. The organ suddenly pealed the mournful strains of *Siegfried's Funeral March*. Was this another tribute to the memory of the departed? The music stopped. I swallowed a cupful of hot black coffee. Such morbid fancies had to cease. I waited until I was certain the Headmistress had had time to return to her office. Then I left the dining room.

Outside, the whirring sound of a vacuum cleaner greeted me. Doors all around the main floor were open now, and there was an air of normal activity about the place. In passing through the corridor, I caught a glimpse of classrooms with their reassuring, even rows of chairs and a desk on a raised platform at the far end of each room.

The door to the Directress' office was open, and I rapped on the walnut panel.

"Come in."

The command was terse. I opened the door wide and stepped into the office. Mrs. Hawkins was standing talking to the Headmistress who was seated behind a high mahogany desk.

"Yes, Miss Evangeline. Quite so. You are absolutely right."

Mrs. Hawkins was a changed woman, obsequious, a veritable Uriah Heep.

"And now with regard to the incident . . ." she went on.

"Another time, Hawkins," broke in the Headmistress. "That will be all for the present."

Our house mother went swiftly from the room. My new employer, with a brief nod, motioned me to a chair near her desk. While she looked through some papers, I had time to study her.

She was handsome in a cold sort of way. Her features were regular and her complexion clear. Her well-shaped head was crowned by glossy, dark brown hair, swept back from her forehead in a stiff pompadour. Her thin-lipped mouth was unyielding, and there was something forbidding and almost otherworldly in those large brown eyes. But hers was the face of an intelligent woman.

She set her papers aside and, without uttering a sound, sat staring steadily at me.

"I had not expected to find you so attractive," she, finally said. "The picture at the agency failed to do you justice."

"Agency pictures are never very flattering," I said.

"We do not engage our teachers for their physical beauty. Here at Meredith Hall we are interested in the spiritual uplift of our students. Physical attraction is subordinated to intellectual achievement."

"Of course . . ."

"Your references are unusually laudatory," she said, after a time. "That is in your disfavor. People who are easily carried away by enthusiasm do not always exercise sound judgment. Then, of course, the majority of the references were written by members of the opposite sex."

I flushed angrily. "I assure you—"

"Please do not interrupt. I did not say that I was not going to employ you. Quite the contrary, Miss Hunter, I have a great respect for ability —my father was a very brilliant man and taught me at an early age to appreciate the value of brains. I am willing to see whether the praise is deserved. Now then, it is settled. You are engaged."

I heaved a very audible sigh of relief.

"As you probably know," she went on, "we accept students of high school age only. To enter here as boarding students, they must be bereft of one parent or completely orphaned. Those were my grandfather's wishes. No one has sought to change them. All day students who can afford the tuition are acceptable. We could not do otherwise without antagonizing the townspeople."

"I think it's wonderful for you to seek out parentless children. You see, I was an orphan, and I—"

"Some other time you will tell me about yourself. Because of the lack of parental supervision, we try to keep our girls under constant surveillance. Each teacher is responsible for a group of ten girls in the dining room. The conversation should be conducted along worth-while channels."

She looked as though she doubted my ability to do this, and then she went on.

"Students are not permitted to go to the village without a chaperone. One day each week it will be your duty to accompany anyone who has a real reason for going to Seacliffe. On Friday or Saturday evenings the students are permitted to attend a motion picture. A teacher must always be in attendance. You will also be required to do dormitory duty one night each week. I tell you these things now so that you will understand when you find yourself listed for the various types of duty. Consult the Bulletin Board at all times."

She paused, then added carefully. "Dates with members of the opposite sex are not permitted among the pupils. Just before the Easter holidays we have a spring dance to which the girls are permitted to invite young men with the proper qualifications. Then, of course, there is the annual Seacliffe Ice Carnival which everyone may attend." Again there was a brief pause while she surveyed me. "Members of the faculty are bound by similar regulations."

"Do you mean that we may not go to town when we please?"

"I mean that your actions must be above reproach."

She lifted a sheet of paper from the desk and handed it to me.

"Here is your schedule of art classes and a list of the students who will attend each one. Miss Vaughn's work books must be in the studio. They will guide you in planning your courses."

I mumbled something about trying to do the best I could.

"One thing more, all your classes will be held in the studio—"

"By the sea?"

The Headmistress nodded and stared at me fixedly.

"Have you already visited the studio?"

"No, no."

I was suddenly unwilling to tell about my experience the night before. A strange expression crossed her face and disappeared almost instantly. I was sure she knew that I was lying. Then she rose majestically and smoothed the creases from her heavy brown dress. I was amazed. I had never seen a woman as tall as Evangeline Meredith and as strong-looking. She was more than regal as she crossed the hard floor to one of the filing cabinets. She removed a small envelope from one of the drawers and handed it to me.

"Here are your keys, one for the front door of the Hall and one for the sea-house. The others are for the closets which contain the art supplies. Since the equipment is costly and valuable, you will find it necessary to keep both the closets and the main entrance locked when you are not in the studio. You will be held responsible if anything is missing. Waste and extravagance are not to be tolerated here."

She returned to the desk, and I knew that I was dismissed.

"Have you any questions before you leave?" she asked as I hesitated at the door.

"When does the school session begin?"

"The faculty will return today. You will meet them at a tea in the reception hall this afternoon. The students return tomorrow. On the following day classes will be resumed."

The dark head bowed once again over the desk, and I left the room.

Well, she was a strange one, but she did seem to know what she wanted. I decided to go to the studio immediately. I would show her that I also knew my business.

A green, turbulent sea met my eye as I neared the studio. I could hear great waves beating the rocky cliff. The cottage was close beside the cliff, as picturesque a retreat as any artist could hope for. As I looked at it, a man came out of the house and down the stone-flagged steps. He seemed lost in thought. His face was handsome but dissipated, and he sported a small, blond mustache. The path was narrow and unavoidably we brushed each other in passing. He lifted his head with a jerk. Bloodshot eyes opened wide. I thought he was going to speak, but he nodded briefly and hurried on. Another strange one!

I climbed the steps, unlatched the door and went into the studio. The anonymous man had come out of it. Why, then had Miss Evangeline insisted on it being locked in my absence?

The sight of the vestibule reminded me of the nocturnal prowler with the green plaid umbrella. Did Miss Evangeline really know about that? Perhaps it had been wrong not to have told her. But it was too late now even for self-reproach.

In the west room I saw that several easels were shoved carelessly against a wall. One of them was broken. A half-empty bottle of turpentine stood near the little modeling stage, and one of the drafting tables was littered with pads and pencils all coated with dust. While I searched the desk vainly for the work books, I found several water colors, each one bearing Eleanor Vaughn's bold signature. It was quite evident that nothing had been disturbed since her death. I opened a window to rid the room of its musty smell. There was a soft meow, and a fat Persian cat jumped in through the window. One of her paws was bleeding. I tried to coax her to me, but she arched her back and looked at me with feline distrust. Perhaps she had belonged to my predecessor, I reasoned, and resented my intrusion.

I continued my search and paused grimly before a half-open closet door. The keys in my pocketbook mocked me. The more I saw, the less I understood my employer's admonishment. I pushed open the door and found large shelves bulging with all the equipment any artist could need.

Upon the floor of this cupboard was a small old-fashioned hope chest initialed *E.V.* in bright gold. I knelt to examine the chest and saw that the lock had been broken. The chest was filled with nothing but sketches. I wondered whether the fair-haired man I had just encountered could have been prying in this chest.

I fastened the closet door and went on to the east room. A soft purr told me the cat had followed. Apparently I had succeeded in gaining her confidence, for she curled up by the fireplace and watched me.

The air in this rom was stuffy, too, and I threw open the window. The room was filled with the roar of the restless sea. I stood listening, captivated by the sound. Suddenly a small slight figure stepped into view. She stood poised on the edge of the cliff. I watched her for several minutes. All at once the form swayed.

"Look out," I called and rushed from the house and down the path toward the crag.

The woman had not heard me, and as I came upon her she was no longer swaying but staring down into the yellow foam as if she were searching for something there. How long she might have remained in that position I do not know, had not the cat, who had followed me once more, opened her pink mouth and emitted an angry wail. The woman wheeled furiously.

"Boots," she screamed, kicking violently at the animal.

"Stop," I cried. "Stop, or you'll kill her!"

The woman turned on me and remained transfixed. The cat limped away.

"Who are you?" she asked, staring in horror at my hair.

Her brown eyes were familiar. She must be Miss Evangeline's sister. But the resemblance ended with the eyes, for there was nothing remotely attractive about this woman. Her complexion was pock-marked and sallow. Her nose was so small it seemed to have been pushed back into her face, and mouselike hair barely covered her ears.

"I'm Nancy Hunter, the new art teacher. I'm to take Miss Vaughn's place."

"*You* are to take Eleanor's place!"

"But Miss Evangeline has engaged me."

"Very well," she said tonelessly. "If Evangeline is satisfied, I must be too."

I sighed with relief.

"I hate cats," she announced unexpectedly, moving away from the cliff. "We'll have to get rid of Boots now."

We started back to the studio together.

As though we had suddenly encountered each other, she informed me, "I'm Helena Meredith." Then, as I mounted the sea-house steps, "You're not going in there?"

"Why, I was. I thought I might go over Miss Vaughn's notes—"

"Let that wait for another day. Leave the studio to her a little longer."

"Very well," I agreed.

But mindful of my new responsibilities, I went inside to close the windows.

She followed me into the east room and hovered over the strange sketch I had discovered on the easel the previous night.

"That was to have been my portrait," she remarked sadly.

I could see the likeness now—the egg-shaped head, the curlless hair, and the nose.

I locked the studio, and we set out for the main house.

"It is too bad you did not meet her," my companion said. "She was so lively, so gay. The students—well, you'll find out how they felt." She laughed quietly to herself. "She was so beautiful, with such soft skin. And her eyes were always dancing."

Miss Helena's hand reached out. She stroked my hair caressingly and murmured. "Just like hers." She dropped her hand sadly and did not say another word.

We ascended the Hall's broad stone steps. As we entered the great hall a tall, brown-clad figure appeared.

"Helena, where have you been?"

"I was just down to the cliff. Down where she—"

"That will do! How often have I told you to keep away from there? Go to your room and rest."

The Headmistress turned to me, her face cold, cruel.

"You will have to pardon my sister. She hasn't been herself since the tragic suicide."

Chapter III

"SUICIDE. . . ."

"Yes, a most unfortunate occurrence. I thought Mrs. Hawkins had told you."

"No, she didn't. But why—"

I saw again that delicate blue handkerchief with its smudge of lipstick, the nail file stuck where a pen should have been . . . Suicide . . .

"There are some questions which are best left unanswered. We feel it unfair to the memory of Eleanor to analyze the motives which prompted her to take her own life. That information was withheld from students and villagers alike for a specific reason. Only the proper authorities know. The reputation of Meredith Hall had to be considered. The school must be protected at all costs. Perhaps you wonder why the suicide of a single teacher might harm us? That goes back into our history. My mother died under similar lamentable circumstances." She paused, her face devoid of expression. "The adverse publicity almost ruined us then."

"But surely people must have been sympathetic . . ."

"I am not asking for an opinion, Miss Hunter. I am explaining a situation so that you might understand our ways and not misjudge us. I will not trouble you with details. Suffice it to say we were involved in disagreeable legal entanglements for a long time. Because of extraordinary circumstances our integrity was questioned. But Aunt Emmeline," here a note of pride crept into her voice, "succeeded in regaining the confidence of the people and freed our name from any taint. I have given you my confidence. You understand that this information is to go no further?"

"I appreciate your telling me this, Miss Evangeline. It will go no further."

"You may go now," she said and went into her office.

I went into my room. With overwhelming relief I discovered that Eleanor Vaughn's clothes and things had been removed. But Eleanor Vaughn still haunted this room. Why had she killed herself?

To get away from my morbid thoughts, I decided to walk to the village and find out why Jeggy Williams had not brought my things.

Once again I went down the driveway, and by the time I had reached the gate I was feeling more like my old self. I noticed a caretaker's lodge at the entrance. I had missed it the night before. An elderly man was oiling the gate, and he swung it open as I approached.

"Is this gate ever locked?"

"Only after ten o'clock at night, Miss."

Peering at me from beneath bushy gray eyebrows he said, "Excuse my staring, Miss, but you do be a lot like her—the lady what died."

My jumbled reply was drowned by the clang of the gate as it closed behind me.

It was a dreary winter day. There was not another house to be seen, only an endless, desolate stretch of vacant field with an occasional stunted tree. But finally I reached a main thoroughfare and at last I came to the village. The dilapidated appearance of the small row of stores that sprawled along Main Street was a sharp contrast to the splendor of the Meredith estate.

In front of the post office, which was a combination Town Hall and police station as well, I found Jeggy and his unmistakable Penelope.

"Miss Hunter, I was jest going to take your things up to the school. Sorry to have delayed, but the car kicked up on me."

"That's all right, Jeggy. I was wondering where I could find you."

"I hang 'round here most of the time. Drive you up to the school now, Ma'am?"

I was about to consent when a church bell reminded me to look at the time. It was one o'clock. Lunch was already being served at the Hall, and if I left now I would arrive too late.

"I think I'll have something to eat here in the village first."

"Sure—you can get something in the drugstore. Take your time. I don't mind waiting."

It was a typical small-town drugstore. I sat down and gave my order. I found myself eating rapidly.

Jeggy had another passenger by the time I came back. She was a garrulous person whom I immediately saw was the village gossip.

"So you're the new teacher, Miss Hunter," she said flaunting the information freshly gleaned from Jeggy. "Well, I'm Mrs. Wilsey."

She extended a bony hand which crushed mine in a quick grip, and without waiting for me to say a word she rambled on, "Sad about the other teacher. Poor girl. I wonder what she died of? Took sudden-like, I expect? There was no epidemic at the school, and Doc Thomas—he lives here in town—says there was no sickness anywhere to speak of." Then, abruptly, "Met George Mundin yet? He's a Meredith on his mother's side." I shook my head, and she immediately gave me a sly poke. "Wait till you do. Oh, my dear, wait till you do. He's the best-looking thing, and they do say a real lady-killer."

I smiled.

"See you again at the Ice Carnival," she sang out as we left her at the edge of a lane just outside the village.

"How does Mrs. Wilsey know so much about the school?"

"Her sister is the school seamstress. She goes up to the Hall most every week and reports back. I don't guess—"

Suddenly, with a noisy sputtering and wheezing the car stopped dead. "There she goes again."

Jeggy looked downright disheartened. He got out of the car and inspected the engine.

A blue roadster drew up beside us, and a dark head leaned out of the window.

"Hello, Jeggy, what's happened? Don't tell me Old Faithful stalled again."

The newcomer's voice was pleasing, and I could see that he was young, although his eyes were melancholy, and there was a cynical twist to his lips. He didn't notice me.

"Afraid so, Mr. James. And we were just taking Miss Hunter and her luggage up to the Hall."

Now the dark eyes looked at me. He nodded coolly and said, "That's unfortunate."

I started to climb out of Penelope. "May I ride up with you?"

"Very well. Come along."

My valises were shoved into the trunk of his car.

"Guess you're all set now, Miss Hunter," said Jeggy. "Good luck."

"Thank you, Jeggy," I said, pressing a bill into his hand.

My companion pressed the starter, slipped quickly into gear, and the car shot forward. The road was a bumpy one, but the driver made no attempt to slow down. Several times I was jostled out of my seat. I looked for a word of apology, but none was forthcoming. From this man's attitude one might have thought he was alone.

I was furious, but I couldn't resist a guarded side glance at his profile. He had a long straight nose and a square resolute jaw. Despite a slight scowl and a morose look about him, he was handsome, and despite his disagreeable manner I found him attractive. But he seemed determined to shut me out.

"I'm sorry to inconvenience you . . ."

"You're not taking me out of my way."

"I arrived yesterday."

"Weren't you a little ahead of schedule?" he asked, turning his full face toward me.

I don't know just what it was, the faint smile that flickered around the generous mouth, or the way his dark eyes pierced through mine, but suddenly my heart began to pound.

"Well," I murmured looking away, "I thought it would be better for me to arrive ahead of the students. After all, when you come to teach in midterm . . ."

"To teach! I thought you were a new student."

I told him my name then and added, "I'm the new art teacher."

"No! You can't mean it. It's too fantastic!"

"I most certainly do mean it."

All signs of friendliness disappeared. He lapsed into his former moody silence and it remained unbroken as we waited for the caretaker to swing open the gate and even as we rode up the steep, curving hill to the Hall.

As the car stopped before the portico I turned to him hesitantly.

"I hope I haven't offended you by anything I said."

"You can't help the situation any more than I."

This was an enigma. There was obviously some preordained barrier between us. Further conversation was prevented by the appearance of the porter who removed our bags. Silently we followed him into the house.

Evangeline Meredith waited for us in the foyer. There was a warm smile on her face as she welcomed Mr. James.

"Philip," she said. "I am glad to see you."

"You're looking well, Evangeline."

"It's lovely to have you back."

"Thank you. It was difficult at first to think of coming back."

"But you belong here, Philip. This is your home."

"Yes, yes, Evangeline, I know." Then, as if suddenly mindful of my presence, "I met Miss Hunter on the road. The car she was in had broken down."

Miss Evangeline turned to me. "If you had told me earlier, the school bus would have been at your disposal. But now let us detain you no further, Miss Hunter. Doubtless you are anxious to do your unpacking."

Philip returned my half apologetic glance with an indifferent one. I moved away, hurt and humiliated. As I started up the stairs I heard him say, "It will be good to be absorbed in work again, Evangeline. I suppose my desk is in order."

Who was this Philip James, and what special position did he hold which entitled him to a private office at Meredith Hall? Most of all I wondered how soon I would see him again. Probably at the faculty tea.

In a half hour I had unpacked my bags and put away my clothes. My few personal belongings made the room less alien.

During my absence someone had righted the oil painting of Emmeline Meredith.

I climbed up on the highboy to take it down once and for all. Just as I had lifted the heavy gold frame from the hook and was in the act of balancing myself on top of the chest of drawers, a voice shouted, "Miss Hunter!"

I had not even heard the door open, but there was no mistaking that voice. It was Miss Evangeline.

"Is Emmeline's portrait so objectionable?"

"It's not that."

"It is settled then. The portrait will remain where it has hung for the past twenty years. You see, this was her room. I cannot help but feel her spirit lingers here to guide her successors."

Toward what end, I thought angrily. Suicide? But I said nothing. Instead I righted the portrait and climbed down. I needed this job. I would have to get used to Aunt Emmeline.

Miss Evangeline crossed to the door and halted upon the threshold. "I think it is only wise for me to tell you before you are carried away by your emotions. Mr. James was engaged to Miss Vaughn."

Chapter IV

IT WAS raining again the morning following the tea. I was depressed, completely depressed. And I was frightened. The tea had been a nightmare. My colleagues had, it seemed to me, gone out of their way to be unfriendly. What was wrong? Could I be held responsible because of a chance resemblance? Could this be the only reason why I was unwanted? And it had not been my imagination which had told me that I was definitely not wanted at Meredith Hall.

I had been nervous at being late, for I had taken more time than I realized in getting ready—having been anxious to look my best. When I arrived, there was an almost audible gasp.

Everyone was dressed somberly. I looked down at my own gown, and myriad eyes followed mine. The bright green seemed to mock me.

Mr. James came slowly forward and politely started to propel me about the room to make introductions. For the moment I was safe.

The faculty members were not many in number, yet somehow as I came in, they gave the impression of a much larger group. All waited to be presented.

In the background was Miss Evangeline dressed in a velvet robe. She had risen from behind the tea table upon my entrance and was now moving majestically about, supervising a servant whenever necessary. She was snubbing me intentionally. This was her way of showing that she was displeased with my dress and angry because of my tardiness, I tried to tell myself.

Mr. James introduced me to a stout woman with graying hair and broad features.

"I am Cornelia Fiske," she said. "Over there is my husband, Homer." She waved toward the fireplace, where a scholarly looking man was bent over the fire warming his hands.

"Mr. Fiske is head of our science department," Philip explained. "He is very much interested in research work in chemical explosives. You must visit his laboratory. It is the round stone building not far from the caretaker's lodge."

More of the faculty, taking a cue from Mrs. Fiske, now joined the little circle we had unconsciously made.

Henrietta Valentine was introduced next. She was the domestic science teacher, slight in stature, eyes watery blue. She was excessively nervous.

"And this is our author, Geoffrey Carter," Philip said, addressing a rather magnanimous-looking man whose graying temples and small mustache gave him a distinguished appearance.

Carter smiled wanly. "I'm afraid Mr. James overestimates my ability. No publisher shares his viewpoint."

I laughed at this, and as I did so, I saw Miss Helena sitting stiffly in a Queen Anne chair. I gave her a friendly nod, but she either did not see it or thought better of returning it.

"Is there any reason why I should not be introduced?" asked someone who offered a flaccid hand.

I looked up. This was the man I had seen emerging from the studio the day before. "I'm George Mundin. Seems like Philip is slow in letting us become acquainted. Can't say I blame you, Phil."

He turned to Philip, but he had moved away. Obviously, there was no love lost between these two.

"And what good fairy, may I ask, was kind enough to leave you here?"

For a brief moment I was caught by the sensual eyes sunk deeply in the handsome but very dissipated face. Some women would have found this man charming. Henrietta Valentine rushed between Mundin and me, nervously chattering.

"As I was just saying to Mr. Carter, it's uncanny—really uncanny —your resemblance to Miss Vaughn."

"But Miss Hunter is far more beautiful," he drawled, watching for the effect of his words on Henrietta.

"Beauty may be a fatal gift."

It was Miss Evangeline. She had moved to Miss Helena's chair to take her empty teacup from her.

Miss Helena whimpered, "She was pretty—far too pretty."

I turned uncomfortably toward her. As I did so, I saw Miss Evangeline's brown-shod foot deliberately lift and stab into her sister's ankle.

"Please have some tea," a Gallic-looking woman offered, handing me a cup. "And help yourself to the little cakes."

Gratefully, I did as she suggested, and she murmured, "I am the French teacher."

At this point, Miss Evangeline asked—then insisted—that I play the piano.

I played two songs—one very emotional and angry and the other gay. My colleagues applauded politely. George Mundin slyly patted me on the arm.

"I teach music appreciation," he said. "If everyone played as nicely there would be more music to appreciate."

"You play very well," Henrietta enthused as she rushed forward to block Mundin from me. "Far better than Eleanor."

Miss Helena stood up.

"It is malicious to suggest any comparisons . . ."

"Excuse me," Philip James said suddenly and walked out of the room.

The silence was unbearable. The tea had gone on somehow, and at last it was over.

Now, as I sat fixing my hair in the dim morning light, I pondered why, when she had been engaged to a man like Philip James, had Eleanor Vaughn taken her own life? The breakfast bell broke in on my musings. I hurried to finish dressing so I wouldn't be late again.

As I approached the staircase, I heard voices coming from a small room in which linens were stored. The voices were Miss Evangeline's and Miss Helena's. Miss Helena was pleading desperately.

"Please don't send me away. I'll do as you want. Only don't send me away again. Please."

"Remember what I told you."

"But you promised. You promised to help me get him."

"Shut up, you fool. Someone may hear us. No one disobeys me. If they even dared . . ."

But Miss Helena was still uncertain.

"What about the new one? Did you see how he greeted her?"

"Didn't I tell you to keep still? Be patient. Everything will work out according to my plan. Besides—there are other ways . . ."

"I'm afraid! You must protect me, Evangeline. You must!" She sobbed convulsively. "If Philip ever knew . . ."

There was a loud, sharp slap followed by a muffled gasp of pain.

"Now get out! And control your nerves! Take the pills Doctor Rudlow brought. They will quiet you."

They were coming from the linen room. I hid among the dim shadows of the passageway.

They went down stairs and I came out of hiding.

Now I knew that something strange, something abnormal and horrible, was going on in this house, and I also knew that I had to find out what was at the bottom of it all. I moved out into the center of the hall and was about to descend the stairs when a voice behind me stopped me.

"You'll find it best to mind your own affairs, Miss Hunter."

It was Mrs. Hawkins.

"You had better go to breakfast," she said levelly. "You're late."

Chapter V

A S I PAUSED upon the landing, the sound of low-pitched voices and occasional giggles was a marvelous antidote for what I had just been through. Looking over the balustrade, I saw small groups of girls crowding the foyer. Their uniform gray wool pinafores and stiff white blouses were an incongruous note in the somber hall. I sensed at once that there was something different about these young people. Laughter was stifled. Smiles were quickly erased. Voices were kept to a whisper.

There was terror in the hunched-over attitudes of these small bodies. There was suspicion in their surreptitious side glances. I did not doubt that their guardians had selected Meredith Hall without consulting their wards. My heart, my unsought sympathy went out to them.

Hundreds of curious eyes stared at me. I had been appraised and, it seemed, found wanting. This was too much. I fled into the nearest class-room and, to my amazement, found a child crouched on the platform near the teacher's desk. She was sobbing heartbreakingly.

"What's wrong?" I spoke gently. "Is there anything I can do?"

A startled, tear-stained face looked up at me, a thin, unhappy face that had a certain piquant charm.

"Oh!" she gasped. "You—you're—"

"Miss Hunter," I said, determined to forestall any further comparison to Miss E.V. "The new art teacher."

The girl struggled to her feet and curtsied.

"I'm sorry . . . I didn't mean to give way, but I—I hate it here, and I wish I were dead."

"You're blue just because it's the first day back at school," I said, drying her eyes with my handkerchief.

"You say that because you've just come. Wait till you've been here a while. Wait—"

"Elaine!"

The two of us wheeled about. Evangeline Meredith stood in the doorway.

"Miss Hunter, we do not encourage such emotional display among our students. Elaine's father has just passed away. Naturally, she is a little more overwrought than usual. Her guardian warned us to expect some difficulty. You may go now, Elaine, but your outings into Seacliffe for the next two weeks will be forfeited."

Elaine received her punishment without a murmur and left the room.

"Some girls," Miss Evangeline continued, "are easily given to com-plaining if they find a willing ear. Such willingness on the part of any faculty member will not be tolerated by me or Mr. James. The students are well cared for. They are all girls of means and can afford the luxuries provided. Any needless dissatisfaction is reported to me at once by the students or faculty."

With this admonition, she swept from the room.

The dining hall was already filled as I entered. I saw at once that Philip was at a table set somewhat apart from the others. Seated with him were George Mundin, Geoffrey Carter, and Helena. Mrs. Hawkins escorted me to a seat.

Hardly had I seated myself when there was the rumbling sound of chairs being shoved away from tables, and students and faculty alike stumbled to their feet. "Good morning, Miss Evangeline," was uttered in chorus. A sign from the Headmistress and places were resumed. Philip pronounced a few words of grace, and then, at last, everyone was per-mitted to eat.

Even today I can still recall the strained atmosphere that prevailed in my corner throughout that meal. The students deliberately avoided my eyes. Elaine's presence at my table saved me from complete ostracism. Unable to bear this hostile attitude any longer, I said, "I'm Miss Hunter, girls, and now you will want to tell me who you are."

Each girl gave her name in a cool, polite voice.

Assuming that this would be the group it would be my duty to chaperone into town, I struggled to make our relationship more cordial by remarking. "You'll have to show me all the Seacliffe sights on Saturday."

"We go on Friday this week."

"There aren't any sights around Seacliffe," put in another girl.

She was very striking in appearance, obviously sophisticated beyond her years. Her slightly reddened lips did not escape me, and I wondered how she managed to have gotten by Miss Evangeline.

"We're third-year students," she informed me loftily, "and we go into the city once a month. It used to be fun with Miss Vaughn."

"Diana," breathed Elaine.

Before anything more could be said, Miss Evangeline gave the signal that breakfast was officially over, by taking a formal departure which caused everyone to rise again. For once I had reason to be grateful to my employer. Now, at last, I would be able to flee from these young tyrants. But, as soon as her sister had gone, Helena Meredith arose, asked us all to be seated once more and read off the activities for the day.

A few muffled and audible groans greeted the announcement that personal inspection would be held immediately in the foyer, preceding the Chapel service. I saw Diana wipe off her mouth with the back of her hand. She caught my eye, and her glance was at once defiant and unafraid. I learned later that she was a potential heiress, and even now received an allowance that was greater than her needs required at the school. This money served advantageously as a bribe for less fortunate students and servants. Diana Marden was going to be a difficult student to handle.

Inspection was conducted in the main foyer where each girl was made to pass before the Headmistress. Some of the girls met with their superior's approval. Others were sent back to their rooms to clean nails, change a blouse or remove rouge from cheeks and lips.

I hesitated irresolutely in the corridor and looked around vainly for other members of the faculty. I was suddenly caught by a fear that my presence might be required elsewhere. Eager to avoid another blunder, I began a search of the classrooms. The round was almost completed when I came upon Philip James writing a series of questions on a blackboard.

"Is there anything special I am supposed to be doing now?"

He turned about and glanced at me in perplexity.

"All the faculty seem to have disappeared," I explained. "I—I was wondering if there was anything I should be attending to before Chapel."

"Good Lord, this isn't a prison, Miss Hunter. You may come and go as you please. Rules are for the students. If you have any preparatory work to do, go ahead. Of course, Miss Evangeline likes the staff to attend Chapel service, but if you don't care to attend, you don't need to."

"I never said I didn't care to attend. It's just that I seem to be the only new teacher here, and no one has taken the trouble to explain the routine."

He hailed Helena as she passed the classroom door.

"Helena, Miss Hunter seems to be in some difficulty. She doesn't know how to spend her time between now and Chapel. Would you help her?"

"I'll be glad to help Miss Hunter," Helena said.

Her elflike face glowed as she looked up at Philip. Did he know, I wondered, or was he blind to the fact that Helena Meredith loved him?

"She's very like Eleanor, isn't she, Philip?" the woman went on, her thin voice a trifle too eager.

"On the contrary, I see no resemblance—other than the color of her hair."

He walked out of the room.

I hated my hair. I hated it.

Helena said, "Why don't you cut your hair off? Everyone comments on it. Why don't you cut it off and make them stop?"

"I'll do it," I said. "Yes, I'll do it. I would even dye it a different color if I had to."

"Cut it off now. Cut it off now while you have the will power. Don't be afraid. I will do it for you, at once, before Chapel. Think what it will be like if you don't, when Evangeline calls you to the altar to present you to the student body."

She led me down the long passage, past the line of girls, up three flights of stairs to her room. The walls, pierced by small, fortress-like windows draped in somber gray, made me realize that I was now in one of the turrets. It dawned on me that this was the room in which I had seen a light burning on the night of my arrival. Had Helena been there at the time? If not, what had Mrs. Hawkins been doing in her employer's room?

My reflections were cut short by Helena's turning the key in the lock of the door.

"We don't want to be interrupted," she explained.

She took a pair of scissors from a sewing basket on top of her bureau. I wanted to run away now, but she pushed me to a chair and pressed me insistently down on the dusty seat. Her fingers dug into the soft flesh of my arm.

"Sit still!"

I was forced to comply as with swift, sure strokes, she began to clip. At last it was over. She stood aside and stared at me.

"They'll never see the resemblance now!"

There was ecstasy in her face and in her voice. Fearfully I got up and went to the bureau. For a long moment I stared at my reflection in the tarnished framed mirror.

"What have you done to me?" I wailed, turning my back on the unbearable sight of that shaggy mop of cropped hair.

I rushed to the door, unlocked it, and ran out into the passage and down the stairs. The concluding strains of the Processional greeted me as I entered the chapel unnoticed and took my place in the nearest pew beside Henrietta Valentine. The choir had already marched to their seats, and Evangeline Meredith at the organ, concluded the hymn with deep-toned resolution.

Henrietta emitted a shocked gasp that caused other heads to turn in my direction. She pressed a hymn book into my hands and whispered, "What have you done?"

I pretended to misunderstand her question and shut my eyes. Then a deep, resonant, familiar voice spoke a few words of greeting. Incensed as I was by his attitude, I could not keep my eyes closed while Philip was talking. I not only wanted to hear him, but I had to see him as well.

After Philip's brief address, Miss Evangeline re-emphasized the traditions of Meredith Hall.

Suddenly I heard my name. Helena had prepared me for this event but, nevertheless, I trembled with stage-fright as I got to my feet.

When I reached the altar I glanced toward the section of the platform where Philip was seated. His forehead was knotted in a heavy frown. My heart sank. Never, I though, would I be able to mount the additional steps to the pulpit, but after Miss Evangeline's brief introduction I found myself facing the student body. Clinging to the reading desk for support, I looked out beyond the long rows of faces, and then I spoke.

"I am happy and grateful to be here with you at Meredith Hall. I know how difficult it is for all of you to accept a stranger in your midst right now, but I hope that before many days have passed, you will permit me to be your friend."

These were the only words I could manage, but unfortunately they appeared to have been ill-chosen.

I was halfway down the aisle to my seat when I heard our Headmistress say, "Since Miss Hunter appreciates our difficult situation, we regret that she considers us unfriendly and trust that she will make allowances for any coolness on our part in the future."

A deliberate slap in the face. She had deliberately tried to set the students against me. The remainder of the service was chaos as far as I was concerned.

Out in the main passage I came upon Philip.

"What have you done?" he asked. "Did you suppose that making a monkey of yourself would help the situation?"

"The sight of my hair seemed to upset everyone. I saw this as a way out of the difficulty, and Miss Helena cut it off for me."

"She should have known better. For heaven's sake, go to the hairdresser this afternoon."

I turned and ran to the faculty closet for my mackintosh and galoshes. I would go down to the studio and try to forget all this in work. The large clock in the hall boomed the hour. It was too late to go upstairs for an umbrella. I would have to borrow someone's. I had just five minutes to make the studio for my first class. With a hurried glance over my shoulder that assured me on one was in sight, I reached into the stand in the corner of the closet, hauled out an umbrella and made for the front door. The umbrella's handle almost slid from my fingers as I stared incredulously at familiar green plaid taffeta. There was no time now to make an exchange, but the whole way down to the art studio, I was tormented by one question. To whom did this mysterious umbrella belong? If I could answer that, I would also know who had visited the sea-house on the night of my arrival. And that, I decided, might be some clue to this whole, wretched, mysterious business.

Chapter VI

I HAD never lived so punctual and rigorous a life as I did at Meredith Hall. I remember now, looking back, how incredibly difficult those first weeks were.

At first I found consolation in the prospect of seeing Philip each day. In spite of his aloofness. At least he did not again evince an antagonistic attitude. But it was not long before even this small comfort was threatened.

It was at one of the many too formal faculty meetings which were held every Wednesday afternoon at four o'clock in the library. The entire staff sat around the huge, shiny, black table.

"It has always been against the school's policy" our Headmistress announced, "for the faculty to be on too intimate terms with the students."

She looked darkly down the row of chairs until her eyes rested on mine.

"Miss Hunter," she said sharply, "I have been told that you are seen frequently with Elaine Barton. And that you have shown partiality to her."

"But the poor child craves affection. She is depressed and lonely. No one—"

"Of course, it is unfortunate that the child of whom you speak is so maladjusted. But you must remember that you are not her private governess. Your attitude, therefore, is quite uncommendable!"

Suddenly I was angry.

"No, Miss Evangeline! It is your attitude that is wrong—"

For a minute there was only the sound of the tick-tock of the big old clock on the mantelpiece. Philip rose and broke the tension.

"Being a sentimentalist, Miss Hunter, does not entitle you to sit in judgment of our ways. I think you owe Miss Evangeline an apology."

With this he closed the meeting.

I had spoken the truth, but I realized that I had gone too far. And humiliated though I was, I knew that I had to make that apology. I did.

About a week later, two incidents occurred which conspired to make my stay at Meredith Hall even more complex and precarious. The first took place one afternoon while Elaine and I were alone in the studio. It was after regular class hours, and Elaine had returned to finish a sketch she had been working on. Since art work was her chief source of pleasure, she spent much of her free time at the sea-house.

This particular afternoon, we were in the west room where a cheery fire was burning on one of the hearths. Elaine was bent over her drawing, shadowing some lines. I went over to the workbench. Elaine looked up and smiled.

"You're so quiet, Miss Hunter. Is anything the matter?"

"No, it's just that sometimes I wonder—about Miss Vaughn."

"What do you mean?" Elaine sounded afraid.

"Elaine, you must know—you spent so much time in the studio— did she ever act strange, despondent?"

Elaine look really frightened, and I took her trembling hand.

"What is the matter, Elaine?" I asked, genuinely disturbed.

The child sobbed wildly. She wrenched her hand from mine and started to tear her drawing to bits.

"Oh, please don't do that!" I begged her.

I realized Elaine knew something and I was determined to have her tell me all she knew.

"When you said good-by to Miss Vaughn before the holidays, did she seem melancholy?"

"We never said good-bye."

Elaine's sobs ceased.

I stared at her questioningly, waiting for her to go on, but she cried out. "Don't ask me any more. Please!"

"Just one more thing. When did you see her last. Why didn't she say good-bye?"

Elaine was strangely silent for a moment as if pondering some important decision. Then reluctantly she said. "Because we were going back to the city together. She was to go with me as far as my father's. The school bus was waiting to take us to the station and when she didn't come downstairs, I went to her room to find her. But she wasn't there."

"You didn't find her in her room?"

"No—only her bag—then I thought perhaps she'd left something at the studio, so I ran down here. I took the path that runs along the cliff. Then I saw—I saw her—"

Suddenly the words choked and her face contorted with fear. She stared at something beyond me. Involuntarily I turned.

Helena stood in the doorway. She glanced around the studio.

"This place is untidy. Remember, Miss Hunter, you are to keep this building clean."

"I did not know it was one of my duties," I answered.

But there was no reply. She had gone as quickly as she had come.

"She's a bully," Elaine whispered. "She takes it out on everyone else because she's bossed by her sister. I hope she didn't hear us talking together. If she did there'll be trouble, you'll see."

"You're so unhappy here. Why does your guardian keep you here?"

"He thinks I'm happy—just as father did. You have no idea how different it is when visitors come. And when you haven't a mother—"

"Yes, I do understand. I am an orphan myself."

"You are, Miss Hunter?"

She was astonished and pleased. This information seemed to bolster her spirit.

"My guardian sent word that he's coming here tomorrow. I'm going to ask him to take me away with him. You must tell him how awful it is here. Please, Miss Hunter?"

I looked at the child's sorrowful face and said, "Yes, dear, I'll see what I can do. I'll find a way to convince your guardian that this is no place for a normal young girl. But now, let's go back to the Hall."

That same night it was my turn to do patrol duty in the dormitories. After making sure that each student was in her bed at nine-thirty, the teacher on duty extinguished the lights, opened the windows, and then took the customary position in the outside hall. Here you were supposed to sit until assured that all the students were asleep. Then one more complete examination of the rooms was to make certain that no flashlights and books were concealed beneath pillows or sheets. Some of the girls would try to read romantic stories in bed.

It was ten o'clock by my watch, when I started to make this final round of inspection. I'd dozed off for a time before making it. The first two dormitories were quiet. Each student was in her place. My light flashed hastily about the third room, past each bed, down the line. Everything seemed all right. But was it? There was something peculiar about a bed in the far corner. I bent over the bed. There was no one there, only pillows and blankets.

It was Diana Marden's bed.

Realizing my responsibility, I nervously made the rounds of the wash-rooms and the other sleeping quarters.

I awakened the girl who occupied the bed adjoining Diana's.

"This is Miss Hunter, Gladys. Diana's not in her bed. Do you know where she could be? I've searched all the other rooms."

"No. I don't. Perhaps she went downstairs."

I went downstairs, but still I found no trace of Diana.

I returned to the front part of the building. There was a light burning in the library. I had forgotten to look there. I gently opened the door and found—Philip. Before I could slip out of sight his head lifted.

"Miss Hunter?"

I backed away hesitantly.

"I suppose you came for a book. Hurry up then and get it."

I was too furious to answer.

He was silent for a moment. Then he said tonelessly. "I'm sorry."

I looked at him, and was no longer angry.

My heart thumped like a sledgehammer. I waited, but he said nothing further. That same insurmountable barrier loomed between us. I turned and ran from the room.

Somehow I got back to the dormitory. Diana was still missing. Perhaps Elaine would be able to help me. I went to her and told her what had occurred.

"I'm not so surprised," Elaine said. "Diana's stolen out before."

"But where could she go?"

She was hesitant. Then she said, "I don't know."

Suddenly I thought of the sea-house and decided to search there.

I ran noiselessly to my room and threw on a coat. I picked up the flashlight from where I had left it on the hall chair, but in my haste, I let it drop. It fell, with a sharp thud. It's glass and bulb broke.

Enough valuable time had already been wasted, so I made for the back stairs. The hall door swung to as I went through, leaving the passageway in utter darkness. I started to descend.

What was that? Someone on the stairs?

"Diana?"

No answer. Still, there was a deeper shadow in the blackness.

"Don't be afraid. I won't report you. Perhaps you had a good reason for going—"

Silence.

I pushed on. Soon I felt a draft and knew that I was nearing the back entrance to the kitchen. Then the door loomed ahead. I went out into the open. The cold wind struck my face.

I was unaccustomed to leaving the building through this exit There was a moon-lit gravel path nearby. I decided to see where it led, and found myself coming out onto the main delivery roadway. Continuing, I passed the now-darkened front of the school and soon came out on the familiar drive. A car turned in at the gate. Its progress was so rapid that I had scarcely enough time to step aside into a clump of bushes.

As a big black sedan sped by, I saw Miss Evangeline and a strange man in the front seat. For that brief moment, by the light of the moon, I caught sight of Helena alone in the rear compartment. She looked strangely ill and wild.

I ran on down the driveway and turned in at the path that led to the studio. I had to find Diana, if possible, before Miss Evangeline learned of her disappearance.

After a futile search, during which I wandered perilously near the sea-cliff edge, I made my way back toward the school.

As quickly as possible, I opened the door and started up the squeaking steps. A door opened, and I felt a draft. A light flashed. Its brilliance blinded me. It was aimed right in my face.

"Where have you been, Miss Hunter?" inquired Miss Evangeline.

"Out—out—taking a walk."

"Walking in this cold wind?"

"Perhaps Miss Hunter was not alone," a voice suggested slyly. "She has been gone for over an hour."

So Mrs. Hawkins had been the one in the passageway.

"What were you doing out at this hour? You know the rules."

Finally as a last resort, and giving up to the fear of losing my job, I explained about Diana Marden's disappearance.

"I can't find her anywhere," I concluded frantically.

Behind the light, Miss Evangeline turned to Mrs. Hawkins.

"What an unlikely story. Have you looked in at Diana's bed at all, Miss Hunter?"

"Of course, but she wasn't there—then."

I could not believe the thought which had suddenly presented itself.

"Under the circumstances," Miss Evangeline was saying, "I think we should go to the dormitory."

The three of us filed silently through the corridor until the dormitory was reached. Mrs. Hawkins still held the light and she flashed it at the bed.

There was Diana, her eyes closed.

"Wait for me in the hallway, Miss Hunter," Miss Evangeline said, "I should like a word with you."

In the hall Miss Evangeline told me I would be penalized two weeks salary, to be paid so much each week into the School Fund.

Chapter VII

A BRISK wind spurred me on as I left the Hall next morning after breakfast and made my way across the frozen ground toward the ridge. A night made sleepless by thoughts of Philip James had left me heavy-eyed and weary. How could he remain at Meredith Hall without realizing the evil it harbored? Unless he too were part of this evil . . .

By the time I reached the ridge the clean fresh air had blown some of the cobwebs from my muddled brain, and I had grown cheerful enough to decide that all was not lost. I still held my job, and by carefully denying myself a few pleasures I could soon make up the money Miss Evangeline was taking from me.

A narrow path led into the woodland where trees were so dense that they formed a shelter in themselves. I looked down. There was a print of a shoe, and it led . . . I stumbled along over the gnarled roots, following the outline of the small, unmistakably feminine shoe. I came out into a clearing. Its pine needle floor was disturbed. A newspaper— yesterday's—was spread over a flat rock. Cigarette stubs, some with a crimson tip, were strewn near by. It was simple to reconstruct the scene that must have taken place the night before. There were other footprints in the clearing, larger, broader ones. A girl and a man had met here. A girl from the school! Diana!

As I returned to the Hall, I saw a town car draw up to the portico. A footman in livery opened the door of the tonneau, and a distinguished-looking, elderly man emerged. He had disappeared within the building by the time I reached the front door, and I had no way of finding out whether or not the visitor was Elaine's guardian save by questioning the driver. I went into the Hall.

Mary was dusting off the dressing table when I slipped into my room. "Well, Miss Hunter," she exclaimed, "you're a sight for sore eyes, but you've been frettin', child!"

"Heavens! It can't be that noticeable," I replied, looking into the mirror.

My face was pinched and drawn. My eyes were glassy, but my hair was beginning to grow longer and the village hairdresser had helped. My hair pleased me now, for I hoped that it would please Philip. Philip —I was in love. Not until now had I dared to admit that to myself, that for the first time in my young life I was in love, and with a man who made it quite plain that nothing would please him more than to have me removed permanently from his sight.

I turned back to Mary.

"You're right. I have been, as you say—'frettin'.' "

"Listen to someone that's older than you," Mary said breathlessly. "Go away, please go away from here, now, before it's too late."

She swallowed hard and went on.

"I heard her talking about you the other day."

"Who? Miss Evangeline?"

She nodded. "Herself. She was talkin' to the other she devil."

"What did she say?"

"Miss Evangeline—"

Hardly were the words out of her mouth when a hurried rap on the door sent the two of us apart.

It was Elaine. She was obviously under a great strain. Something out of the ordinary was taking place, for she wore a handsome green velvet dress in place of the drab school uniform. Her large blue eyes looked at me imploringly as, grasping my hands, she cried.

"My guardian, Mr. Morgan is here. He's downstairs in her office now, and you've got to speak to him. You promised."

"How long is he staying?"

"Just for today. And he's taking me off somewhere for lunch."

"Then we'll have to act quickly."

My first class was scheduled for eleven o'clock.

"Wait here. Don't come down with me. Give me a few minutes alone with your guardian before you join us."

As I reached the bottom of the stairs the office door opened, and Miss Evangeline herself stood before me.

"Why, Miss Hunter, I was just coming in search of you."

She seized my arm so tightly that it hurt, the set smile never wavered on her face, and she led me into the room.

"Here she is, Mr. Morgan. Here's the young lady about whom I was just telling you."

The distinguished-looking man I had observed outside rose to greet me. He extended a cordial hand.

"Do sit down, young lady," Mr. Morgan said. "Miss Meredith has been telling me how fond you are of my ward. That pleases me very much."

"She is so solicitous of the child's welfare, the other students are jealous." Miss Evangeline said sweetly.

"I can't tell you how relieved I am to hear this," Mr. Morgan said when my employer had concluded a further account of my remarkable devotion to Elaine. "The child was so broken up by her father's death that I was deeply concerned over her welfare."

At this point Miss Evangeline left us alone.

"I'll find Elaine," she said, with a glowing smile.

"It is not easy to be in my position," he said after a pause.

"Of course not," I agreed, seeing this as an opening wedge for what I had to say. "It's important that a sensitive child like Elaine be placed in the right environment."

"Yes, yes," he agreed. "Persons like yourself are far better able to handle the girl's problems than I would—"

"Mr. Morgan, I beg to differ with you. This is not the ideal place for your ward. She hates it here!"

"Surely you are joking, Miss Hunter."

"I was never more serious in my life. Elaine is unhappy here."

"Unhappy—ridiculous. Elaine's devoted to you, isn't she? Of course. Well, isn't it natural for her to wish to remain where you are?"

He had me there. Our Evangeline had scored again. By painting such a happy picture of the relationship between Elaine and me nothing I could say would shake his belief that Meredith Hall was the place where the child belonged.

At the studio, I found Diana. She made no pretense of having come ahead of the others because of any sudden industry.

"How dare you spy on me?" she demanded.

"I don't understand, Diana . . ."

"Yes, you do! Why did you have to make a row about last night?"

I sat down at my desk.

"If you are referring to my anxiety over your disappearance last night, I'm sorry you feel that way."

"Your anxiety . . . That's a laugh! You're not worried about anyone but Elaine."

"Diana, won't you try to be friends? I only want to help you."

"You can help me best by staying out of my affairs. If you don't, you'll be sorry."

The other girls poured into the room at that moment. They were in time to hear Diana's last words. I caught sight of the smirking faces of Marjorie Jonas and Eliza Horning, Diana's special satellites. And of Gladys, Diana's lanky room mate.

"I am sure when you reconsider what I have told you, Diana," I said quietly, "you will change your attitude."

"I'll never change toward you!"

I realized that I had allowed the discussion to progress too far and said no more but attempted to prepare for class.

That morning, by popular request, we were beginning portraiture. I permitted each student to select her own model from the members of the class.

For some time I allowed them to work uninterruptedly, and then I quietly walked up and down the aisles between the tables, offering suggestions to one and criticism to another. When I reached Diana's side I found her canvas blank. She had not even begun to sketch in an outline but was sitting there stroking Boots, who purred contentedly on her lap.

"Doesn't this type of painting interest you, Diana?"

"What do you know about painting? You're just a sham!"

She shoved her chair away from the easel.

"We don't want you here!"

Eliza Horning, Marjorie Jonas, and other student-followers of the glamorous Diana took up the cry shouting, "We don't want you!"

"I hate you," cried Diana. "Oh! Why did she have to die!"

It seemed impossible to restore order, nor did I know how to cope with this situation.

In the midst of this wild excitement I saw Philip James in the doorway. The slightly indolent way in which he leaned against the doorpost told me he had been there for some time.

"Class is dismissed!" I shouted.

"Wait," said Philip, having finally made up his mind to take part in the proceedings.

Startled "Oh's!" and "It's Mr. James!" filled the air.

"I have just heard a most reprehensible little scene. I think I know who instigated it, and—"

Before he could go on I stepped forward a trifle breathlessly.

"Please. They didn't mean anything, Mr. James. They were just wrought up emotionally—it's nothing . . ."

"Very well, girls," Philip said, "if Miss Hunter is willing to forgive and forget I will not stand in her way."

The bell sounded from the chapel. With a haughty toss of her head and a defiant glance in my direction, Diana led the exodus from the studio. I sank wearily into the nearest chair, staring blindly out of the window, wanting only to be left by myself to allow the wounds to heal.

"I've tried everything. It's no use. They just don't want to like me."

"Eleanor Vaughn always made a great fuss over them," Philip said, half to himself, "particularly Diana. And she is the ringleader. Of course, Eleanor was the type of person who becomes very popular. You see she was so gay, so lively, always planning something to keep the girls amused on the night she was in charge of activities. It was charades or . . ."

"I suppose you think I've failed utterly as a teacher."

"No, I recognize what you are up against in trying to take her place. It's unfortunate that the students have assumed such an unfriendly attitude. I will speak to the girls again, or perhaps Evangeline had better . . ."

"Oh, no!" I broke in hastily, "please don't tell Miss Evangeline about this."

"Very well," he said.

As he started for the door I found time to wonder what had brought him to the studio in the first place. As though some mental telegraphy had passed between us he spoke suddenly.

"It's the first time I've been to the studio since—since the holidays. Nothing is changed, nothing is changed."

"I left everything just as I found it. I thought everyone would want it that way."

"Yes, I suppose they do—"

He broke off abruptly, and passed a hand over his forehead.

"I came down here especially to see you," he said, "about last night. I wanted to tell you that I had not intended to be so abrupt in the library."

He went swiftly away.

Long after the door closed on him, I stayed in the studio, clinging tightly to a chair to still the trembling of my body. The events of the morning had been too much. First Elaine, then Diana, and now Philip. His whole attitude bewildered me, but over and over I kept repeating to myself, "He apologized. He apologized."

Why he had done so I could not imagine.

At luncheon I learned that Elaine had gone off with her guardian and would not be back until the late afternoon. And the incident in the studio, having somehow failed to make the dormitory grapevine, the students treated me with their normal indifference.

The day wore on slowly. I could hardly wait until my last class ended, but at last I stretched out on the bed and fell into a heavy doze. I awakened to find myself being shaken roughly.

"Miss Hunter! Oh! Miss Hunter, please wake up."

"What's wrong, Elaine, child, tell me."

I drew her down on the bed beside me and smoothed the crumpled velvet dress while she spoke.

"Mr. Morgan is going to Shanghai, on business—and he's leaving me here until he comes back."

"Couldn't he take you with him?"

"No-o. I begged him. I told him I wouldn't be a bit in the way. He said Father never took me along on his travels, and that girls of my age are better off in a school. But I'm afraid. I don't want to stay here. I'd rather be dead." She sat bolt upright at this and reiterated, "I'd rather be dead."

"Elaine," I said sternly, "you must pull yourself together. I'll tell you what. You've had such a trying day, suppose I try to get special permission for us to go to the moving pictures tonight."

She sobbed more quietly now. "Don't leave me alone with them. Don't—ever—"

"I won't, and when the summer comes the two of us will visit my aunt. Julian will be glad to have someone else to talk to, and you'll have a nice holiday."

"If only they will let me go."

"Why shouldn't they?" I asked, knowing that there were a million excuses Miss Evangeline might find. "Now, change your clothes while I go down to get permission from Miss Evangeline."

"No," cried Elaine, "not Miss Evangeline. That would never do. Please don't ask her! Ask Mr. James. He might let us go."

No light was visible beneath the door of Philip's office, but I knocked.

"Is there anything I can do for you, Miss Hunter?"

I had not seen Evangeline and, as usual, she startled me. I had changed my mind about wanting to tell her anything.

"No—nothing."

"Mr. James is not in his office."

"Do you know when he will return?"

"He does not keep me posted as to his goings and comings."

She swept majestically away into the library.

The gong sounded for supper, and the girls began pouring out of the study hall and down the stairs. Their high voices filled the air as they whispered and chattered among themselves.

While I tried to decide what to do, the library door opened, and Philip emerged with Miss Evangeline. It was impossible to approach him then. I followed the girls into the dining hall. Elaine was tardy, and as she took her seat there was a question in her red-rimmed eyes.

"Not yet," I said softly.

Diana heard the remark, and I knew that her curiosity was aroused.

Immediately after supper I took Elaine aside and explained what had happened. At that moment I saw Philip step into the corridor, and after telling Elaine to wait for me in my room, I hurried after him. He suggested we go to his office.

I felt at home in Philip's office at once. On this, my first visit, I noted how similar his quarters were to Miss Evangeline's in shape and furnishings, but there the likeness ended. It had a lived-in feeling. Above all, there was the comforting, manly smell of tobacco.

"Now, what can I do for you?"

Briefly I explained the purpose of my visit, not failing to paint a true picture of Elaine. Her fears he brushed aside.

"Childish emotionalism," he said, "and you should not encourage her to think along these lines. Not but what I believe you are right about the child's needing some diversion," he added. "You have my permission to take her to the movies. It seems to me there's no harm in that."

Just as I was thanking him, Miss Evangeline came into the office and, before I could get away, Philip had explained the nature of my visit.

"Ah-h-h-h, Miss Hunter, is this then what you referred to as 'nothing'?"

I did not answer.

"Perhaps," Miss Evangeline offered lightly, "Miss Hunter does not know that it is customary to consult me on all such matters. You see," she explained sweetly, punctuating her phrase with a forced, musical laugh, "we make it a point of not troubling our Mr. James about trivialities." Then she turned to him. "I'm afraid, Philip, Miss Hunter felt that you would be more susceptible and hence more lenient."

How well she knew people. This comment was just the sort to antagonize a man like Philip and turn him against me. He muttered something about preferring not to be involved in unimportant school matters.

"In the future," he said to me, "please take these matters up with Miss Evangeline. Hasty decisions are usually bad, and I haven't the time to delve into the individual problem of each student. Perhaps you know the whole situation better than I, he told the Headmistress. "I'm quite willing to leave the matter up to you."

"Thank you, Philip. You have decided sensibly. Miss Hunter is new in our ways and doesn't understand your request to be free to pursue your own work." Then she turned to me. "I see no reason for breaking a steadfast rule."

She crossed to the bell-pull by the door and jerked it swiftly.

"It will be far better for Elaine to retire early. Perhaps she would prefer to be alone tonight. I will have a room prepared for her upstairs."

At that moment I was so furious at Philip, so enraged at the man's gullibility that I could have committed mayhem without batting an eyelash. Mrs. Hawkins came in.

"You rang for me, Miss Evangeline?'"

"Yes. Tonight Elaine is going to sleep in the Green Room."

She seemed to pause pointedly before going on.

"She is to be left entirely undisturbed, but you may see that she has a warm drink before retiring."

"You may be sure that I will see that she is properly taken care of."

"Yes, Mrs. Hawkins, I know I can always count on you."

Then Mrs. Hawkins said, "When you are free, Miss Evangeline, Diana Marden is waiting in your office."

That was the first inkling I had that Diana was to be punished.

"Tell Diana I will be with her directly," the Headmistress said.

The housekeeper hurried from the room, and Miss Evangeline turned again to Philip.

"Excuse me, Philip. Will you be free later? There is a matter of expenses I would like to discuss with you."

"You'll find me in the library."

Philip and I were alone once more.

"Mr. James," I began uncertainly.

He broke in harshly, "I'm afraid that you have been presuming on a well-intentioned apology I made this morning. It was meant as an apology and not as a prelude to anything further."

I ran from the room and up the stairs.

A short time later Elaine joined me in my room. One look at my face told her the story. I hadn't received permission.

Chapter VIII

"I'D BETTER go back to the dorm," Elaine said. "I have some algebra to do."

"Elaine," I said on impulse, "why did Miss Vaughn get along with the girls so much better than I do?"

This question upset Elaine. She thought a long time before giving me an answer.

"Diana always liked Miss Vaughn because she was lenient."

"Lenient! Then how did she manage to get along so well with the authorities?"

She said in a rush, "Watch out for Diana. She's dangerous."

So the news of the morning's episode had at least spread. I took a deep breath and asked, "What do the other girls think of the incident in the studio? Are they in sympathy with Diana?"

"A good many are. They're just like sheep! Diana thinks for them and even pays for their liking her. I told them all I thought Diana's conduct was shameful. I'm sure some of the girls agree with me, but they're afraid to say so. They know Diana's one of Miss Evangeline's favorites. Right now she's bragging about how lightly she got off after last night."

"How do you mean, lightly?"

"Do you know about the School Fund?"

"No. What's that got to do with punishment?"

Elaine came back into the room and sat down on the arm of the winged chair.

"Miss Evangeline is a miser. She loves just two things—money and Meredith Hall—the building, not the people in it. She established a special School Fund to be used for improvements—new equipment and that sort of thing. Whenever a girl is caught breaking certain rules she can escape punishment by putting money into this fund."

"It doesn't seem possible. How does she get away with such a plan—it's blackmail!"

"In a way it is, but she's smart. She makes it look as though we benefit by it. You see, the contribution is voluntary. We can make it or accept the consequences. Punishments depend on how bad we've been. It may be cancellation of special privileges for a time, or," here her voice grew tense, "having to sleep in the Green Room."

"The Green Room?"

"It's a room on the top floor. Being sent there's the worse punishment . . . I've never been. I think I'd die if I did—but other girls have gone and then been sick for days. They say the room is haunted, and . . ."

Someone knocked on my door. I managed a feeble, "Come in."

The door was instantly flung open, and Mrs. Hawkins came in

"Sorry to disturb you, Miss Hunter, but Miss Evangeline sent me to fetch Elaine."

"Why? What does she want?"

"You'll soon find out. Better come along without a fuss, if you know what's good for you."

Elaine cast a fleeting, imploring glance in my direction. I wanted to help her, but there was nothing I could do.

I tried desperately to sleep, but I could not close my eyes. It was not only of my own situation that I was brooding, but I suffered for Elaine. I was furious when I recalled how deftly Miss Evangeline had conveyed the impression that she was doing Elaine a great favor by sending her to the Green Room.

The longer I thought the more convinced I became that I had to go to Elaine, that I had to stay with her until she fell asleep.

I slipped into my robe and stole into the silent corridor. It looked vast. For an instant I clung to the brass doorknob as somewhere below a clock chimed midnight. Then I reached out for the wall. There was a stir followed by a heavy rushing on the other side of the plaster. Rats . . . My flesh crawled. I snatched my hands from the wall and groped along the passage.

There wasn't a sound save my heavy breathing, but the night played queer tricks on me. Unseen eyes seemed to be watching. Someone was waiting for me a few feet ahead. Someone so quiet, so tall and sinister. Perhaps I could slip by that figure unnoticed. I edged carefully to one side, holding my breath. I passed it! Suddenly I couldn't move. Someone clutched my kimono. Someone was drawing me back slowly, slowly. I thought I heard a hushed whisper. With a jerk, I wrenched off my robe and dashed ahead. Someone was following, but I kept on running until I reached the hall door. I tried opening it, but it wouldn't give. My fumbling fingers found the key in the lock and very carefully I opened the door.

A draft from somewhere greeted me. I shivered in my thin nightgown. Somewhere above a door closed, and then the air was still. I waited for a moment. No one was following me now. Leaving the hall door open, I crept toward the stairs. I reached the landing and then realized with a sick feeling that I had not the faintest idea of the Green Room's location. My only visit to these upper regions had been with Helena, and we had gone directly to her room.

I turned back toward the stairs, and there I halted. With Elaine lying alone and terrified, I could not go back. Then there was only one thing for me to do. Helena and Mrs. Hawkins both occupied rooms on this floor. One of them would have to be consulted. But I did not know which was the house mother's room and so had no choice. Without any further hesitation, I went along the hall to the room I remembered too well and rapped softly on the door. There was no answer. I knocked again and waited. Finally, ready to assume any risk, I went in. The moon had fully emerged. The bed was empty.

Where was Helena?

Suddenly someone screamed dreadfully. The terrible sound snuffed out like a candle. It was not repeated. Then the door behind me opened. Helena Meredith, clad in a white nightgown, her eyes wide open, yet filled with the awful, vacant stare of the somnambulist, stood there.

She closed the door and leaned against it for an instant while a guttural sound escaped her lips. Then she spoke, not in her usual timid way, but loudly and forcefully.

"Philip, Philip, where are you? You're going to be mine. Do you hear? You and I and Meredith Hall. Then we'll put Evangeline in her place."

For an instant the very mention of Evangeline's name terrified her, and she stretched out her arms as if to ward her sister off.

"No, no. This time you can't get me. When I'm Philip's wife, I'll be out of your reach, and who knows . . ."

When she got into her bed, I opened the door and stepped out into the hall. Simultaneously the door across the hall opened, and as Mrs. Hawkins came out I slipped back into the shadows to escape the gleam from the lamp burning inside. She turned on the light over the stair and, hurrying down, disappeared through the open doorway.

Excited murmurs came from the hall below. People were moving about in the main building. The dormitory had been aroused by the piercing cry.

Then I heard Miss Evangeline's voice, calm, unshaken.

"Go back to bed, all of you. Nothing is wrong. Someone upstairs had a bad dream."

A voice rose hysterically, "It's Elaine in the Green Room."

Then the anxious voices faded as many doors closed. I heard our Headmistress speak again. This time her voice was much closer. She was very near my part of the building, and I heard her speaking angrily to someone.

"Who opened that door? Haven't I warned you to see that it stays shut?"

"I closed it myself, Miss Evangeline, and locked it. I can't imagine who passed through here."

I recognized the second voice as belonging to our house mother.

"Do you think she did it out of spite?"

Who was she, I wondered. Elaine?

"I don't really know, Miss Evangeline. She was in a vicious mood this evening until I gave her the medicine."

Now I was certain they were referring to Helena, but I had no time for further eavesdropping. I had to act fast if I wanted to reach Elaine before Mrs. Hawkins returned to her room.

I tore swiftly down the hall in the direction from which I thought the scream had come. Of four doors, mercifully, I selected the right one and went anxiously into the room.

I saw another empty bed in a small, windowless room. Then I saw a huddled white form on the floor. I ran to the child. Someone said, "So it's you, Miss Hunter."

I looked up into Miss Evangeline's wrathful face.

"I told you I wouldn't trust her," said Mrs. Hawkins.

"So," went on Miss Evangeline, "you not only eavesdrop, but you spy as well."

She looked at my scantily-clad body.

Had she pulled my kimono from me? There seemed to be an answering flicker in her eyes as though she had read my thoughts.

"Please, can't all that wait? This poor child's unconscious!"

I bent over the still form once more. The heartbeat was feeble.

"Quick," I cried, "we must get her back to bed—but not in here. She needs fresh air."

During the next half hour there was no time for conversation. We were all too busy with Elaine. The two women were so disturbed over her condition that my instructions were carried out hastily.

For a time it seemed that we had lost her.

"Elaine," I cried desperately, "darling, wake up. It's Miss Hunter, Miss Hunter!"

How often I repeated these words I do not know, but finally they were answered by a slight moan. The eyelids fluttered and finally lifted. Then she sat up with a jerk and screamed, perspiration pouring from her body. I tried to calm her.

"Miss Hunter . . ."

I had to strain my ears to catch the words.

"I saw it. I saw it."

Her voice began to rise.

"Don't let them send me back. Stay with me! Don't let them send me back!"

When Elaine at last was quieted, Miss Evangeline prepared to leave and ordered me to accompany her. I begged to be allowed to remain at the girl's bedside.

"She will not awaken until morning. Mrs. Hawkins dissolved a grain of amytal in the glass of water Elaine drank."

I followed Miss Evangeline from the room and down the stairs. She closed the hall door, locked it and slipped the key into her pocket. I knew that in the future no one would be able to steal up to the third story. She did not go on to her room but instead led me to mine and came inside. She shut the door and wheeled on me.

"Why did you go upstairs?"

"I thought Elaine had endured enough without being frightened to death."

"Why should she be frightened?"

"The other girls told Elaine that the Green Room was haunted."

"And you believed a story concocted by childish minds?"

"I—"

"You must have, to be in such haste to get upstairs."

I followed her glance to my bed. There was my kimono, and even at a distance I could see a great rent in the skirt where the material must have caught on some hook in the hall.

"I had not expected you to be so credulous."

"I think I've found their ghost," I said.

"You're sure you're not letting your imagination run away, as you must have when you left your robe in the hall."

"Yes, I'm quite sure. I saw your sister. I was in her room."

"You have a crippled cousin, Miss Hunter, of whom you are very fond."

"What has he to do with it?"

"He needs an operation. You hope to provide the money."

"Yes, I do."

"It would be unfortunate if you found yourself without a position and unable to procure one anywhere. After all, it is essential that a teacher be perfectly normal—"

"What are you trying to tell me?"

"Elaine was frightened by a nocturnal visitor whom she assumed was a ghost. You were caught prowling in a part of the building where you do not belong. I hardly think anyone would consider that the rational thing to be doing. Of course, Mrs. Hawkns, my sister Helena and I would be bound to reveal our suspicions to the proper people. However," she smiled, "if you manage to restrain your impulsiveness in the future, we will consider tonight's incident closed."

She went away.

I closed the door and turned the key carefully in the lock. But I knew that I was trapped. I knew that Miss Evangeline had me trapped.

Chapter IX

WHEN the midterm examinations had ended, classes were suspended for three days before the beginning of the new term. Many of the faculty members went into the city, but I did not want to spend any unnecessary money.

Late on one of the holiday evenings I sat alone in my room writing to Julian, when there was a knock on my door. It was Cornelia Fiske. I was surprised, for I had thought that all the faculty had gone away. I said as much.

"What is the point of going away from here just long enough to have Mrs. Hawkins go prying through our things!"

"I don't understand . . ." I said.

"You see, none of us is invulnerable. We are all spied upon subtly but ruthlessly by the powers-that-be. We are here under peculiar circumstances—hardly desirable ones—and nothing can be done about them."

"Please tell me what is going on here. Please tell me why everything seems so monstrous, so cruel. I hate all this—the lies—the scheming—the devilish spying that goes on . . ."

"Yes, yes, indeed," she agreed amiably. Her sudden change of tone made my outburst sound foolish. "You are quite right, my dear. But those are Meredith traits, characteristic of my dear departed uncle, and all the other Silas Merediths. I know them well—you see we are almost all Merediths here. But . . . you don't know about our ancestry. Perhaps you would like to learn."

She beckoned me toward the door.

"Come with me, Miss Hunter. It might be a good thing to tell you about the history of our precious school and its background. Everything ties up with the late Silas Meredith's will, and you will see an excellent likeness of that old devil there."

Mrs. Fiske laughed metallically.

"But—better still—I'll take you down to the family chantry. It lies under the chapel. There you will not only see portraits of all the Merediths—but you will have the singular honor of beholding all but one of their actual tombs—even my father's. Of course," she peered at me and her eyes held that same look, "it is only because I am interested in you that I show you these things. This family burial place is rather a well-guarded secret, and the entrance to it is always dark as pitch. We'll need a lamp. Evangeline always takes one with her. She often goes there to pray and to commune with the departed. They say that she has even had her own tomb all prepared for her, but as yet no one has been able to find it."

Why did she want me to go down in the family's secret vault? What would I have to do in return? But I had to go. I had to find out what was really going on. I got a lamp and followed Cornelia Fiske out into the dimly lighted passageway and along toward the main hall that led to the back stairway.

"I'll take the lamp," she said. "You'll be able to follow more easily."

She led me through a remote part of the building. After a time, the passageway narrowed and then suddenly stopped. She found a button upon the wall and pressed it. A portion of the interior drew slowly back on quiet, well-oiled hinges and a damp, musty odor hit us. For a moment, Mrs. Fiske stood motionless on the threshold. Then with a low whisper she told me to follow her into the remote, dank recess which lay beyond.

Our steps took us down an iron stairway. Down, down, we went into that hideous hole. At last Mrs. Fiske flashed the lamp about, and I saw that we had arrived at the entrance to some sort of cathedral-like chamber. I heard rats scampering.

We moved up a flight of large stone steps until we were on a rocky plateau. Here many grotto-like passages clustered. These small cavern-like retreats were covered by arches which heightened the grandiose effect of the entire chamber. Nor were these vaults the most singular feature of this chamber of death. The light seemed to come from nowhere and yet be focused somehow upon each sarcophagus. I shivered because I was cold and because I was frightened.

Mrs. Fiske stopped before an imposing stone coffin and stopped to rest the lamp upon the cold marble.

"This is where the first Silas Meredith lies."

Then as she continued speaking she took from a pocket in her skirt a piece of candle which she lit with the aid of the lamp. She crossed the room with the candle and lit a second cylinder of wax which was concealed by a small metal shell at the bottom of a bizarre-looking fresco. The gleam from the sheltered light glimmered weirdly upon a large, antiquated painting, hitting directly the eyes of the man who stared sternly down upon us. There was an evil expression about those eyes, an expression pregnant with avarice and excessive cruelty.

"The first Silas settled along these shores about 1830. He was forced to flee from England. Nevertheless, he prospered considerably in the new world and began to build a manor of his own. He liked the power that wealth must bring—as all of us do—and visualized himself a mighty baron with vast estates." A note of pride was creeping into her voice. "He built the original part of this building out of the wood and stone that could be gotten near by. He constructed these catacombs and the subterranean passage that leads to the stone house. Just before his death, he enlarged this crypt so that it would extend under the family chapel which he erected as a memorial to himself and which we still use today."

"Mrs. Fiske, why, with all their wealth, have the Merediths continued to run a school?"

She hesitated for a fraction of a second, and then said slowly, "Perhaps, being a member of the family, I should not tell you this, but . . . it goes back to the first Silas Meredith. He never had any education. After he had amassed his fortune, he found that he was shunned by leaders of society. When he died he stipulated in his will that a school was to be founded at Meredith Hall. To make certain that he would not meet with another sort of rebuff here, he opened the school doors only to orphaned boys of means. In those days, only members of the male sex were thought worth educating, so it became an academy for boys. From that point on, the Merediths made their mark in the field of education. No one has looked down on them since.

"When Uncle Silas died—that was Silas the third—he left the main part of his estate to his daughters and Philip James. But he stipulated that if one of them should ever leave the school, that one would lose his income from the school, and it would be divided between the other two."

"Philip James!" I exclaimed. "Is he related to the Merediths?"

"Oh, I thought you knew. That is, he is related by marriage. You see his mother was Uncle Silas' second wife and Uncle Silas became very fond of Philip. He adopted him legally long before he died."

I wanted to ask a thousand questions more but Mrs. Fiske talked on rapidly.

"Into one of the additions he had built, the first Silas included a dark dungeon-like room which is now being used as a pantry to the kitchen. You have probably seen it. He kept this awful hole down here also as a threat to his beautiful wife whom he suspected of infidelity. Not that I would have blamed her . . . the first Silas Meredith was insanely jealous and unbearable. Then, there was the eldest son who inherited all the old man's weakness and added a few eccentricities of his own. He was the second Silas. Then there was Andrew, Silas the second's brother, who later had a daughter named Deborah."

We moved into the adjoining chamber. She extinguished each candle as we went along.

"This is the second Silas Meredith. He had three children."

She followed my glance as it traveled to a magnificent statue of Emmeline, the great idol of the school, whose picture hung so resolutely in my bedroom.

"Silas the second bequeathed about all of his part of the family fortune —and the school—to his sister Emmeline and his favorite son, Silas the third. Georgia and Samuel, his other children, were more like their mother, not as strong and aggressive as their brother, and were subsequently left almost penniless." She spoke bitterly again, resentfully. "They always suspected that they had been cheated by their brother. It seems that down through the generations the Merediths have always aligned into two groups, the aggressors and those who sought appeasement."

The bitterness of my companion's tone caused me to peer more closely at her. I saw a new Cornelia Fiske, 'a woman who possessed latent strength and a strong streak of devout family pride.

I listened more intently as she talked.

"Andrew Meredith, my uncle, had only one daughter, Deborah. Silas the third was shrewd enough to marry her—she was his cousin. In that way he thought to gain control of all the family fortune. Silas had two daughters of this union—Evangeline and Helena. Evangeline seems to have inherited all the strength of the Merediths but Helena is more like her mother."

Here Cornelia Fiske gave a little snort.

"There was never any love lost between Silas and Uncle Andrew, but for a while things were peaceful. However, when Andrew died he left all his money to Evangeline. I often wondered if he did it because he hated Uncle Silas. He left the money in trust so neither Silas nor Deborah could touch the principal. Silas forced Deborah to contest the will, but to no avail. They say the strain of the litigation made Deborah kill herself. I wonder!"

Cornelia was warming toward her topic.

"Deborah's suicide brought about a decline in the school's popularity. But Great-aunt Emmeline saved the Hall," she said proudly. "It was her quick thinking that closed the academy for a time, then later opened it up as a girl's school. Evangeline is like her in some respects. I have to admit that. Well, to go on—but then . . . you are shivering, Miss Hunter, perhaps we should go back upstairs?"

"Not yet, please . . ."

"Well, anyway, Georgia, the next eldest offspring of the second Silas, married and moved away from here. Later she had a son and called him George. His last name is Mundin, as you know."

So that explained another member of the faculty!

Mrs. Fiske moved into another small room and lit a candle.

"Here is a picture of Georgia. She never had a .statue made and is not buried here. Samuel also left the Hall and later married and had a daughter who, upon her marriage to a college professor, became me, Mrs. Cornelia Fiske. My father is interred over there. I put that expensive painting over his tomb. It is well protected from the damp by its frame and glass."

She halted to catch her breath.

"Silas the third hated his two daughters, primarily because he had wanted a son to keep the Silas Meredith line going. He and Evangeline

were so much alike that she continually infuriated him. Perhaps he could
have forgiven the same characteristics in a male but not in a woman.
And yet he despised Helena, too, for being the very antithesis. So he
adopted Philip, and to curb his daughters' power, he inserted a clause
in his will that the children of Georgia and Samuel as well as the instructors he had chosen were to hold some position at the school for
life if they so desired. Reversed circumstances and the folly of old
age made us return."

She was suddenly silent. Then she said loudly, "There is the old
devil's coffin, in that crypt. He was a clever man, despite his faults. Silas
knew, too, that we all were education minded and that most of us had
taken up the teaching profession. So you see, that is how we all came
to be here, and—George and I are cousins of the two Meredith sisters."

"But must you remain at the school?" I persisted, coming back to
the original problem. "Haven't you saved any money?"

Cornelia was quiet for a moment and then said, "Not enough—my
husband requires so much to carry on the research work that he is
doing. He is trying to find a new, more economical, safer explosive.
Besides," she went on angrily, "my father, Samuel, had a right to the
Hall, too. Evangeline likes to think of us as charity. But we aren't!
Everyone here's a slave to money . . . I suppose that is the reason you
are here?"

"Yes, this is the first position that has paid anything worth while."

Then I went on to explain about Julian and about my early life. "So
you see," I ended up, "I, too, have to stay."

"Greed and the never-ending fight for life always change people," she
said. "Like the time that Silas' will was read. You should have seen
their faces—the Merediths and some of the others. Homer and I were
not expecting much, you understand, for ourselves—but we knew that
there had been a split somewhere.

"According to Silas' plan, George and I were the two poor relatives
mentioned in the will. He knew that we had never gotten along too
amicably with Evangeline. It was all part of the hellish scheme. If we
outlived Evangeline and Helena, George and I were to share a portion
of the estate. George, after all, was the only male in the family proper.
It's ironical that the one who seized almost everything from us had no
male descendants to carry on."

"How about the others?" I asked. "How did they manage to be
caught here?"

"Henrietta Velentine had been working at a charity school when the
old man, on an inspection tour of such institutions, took a liking to her.
Geoffrey Carter wrote books on education and was practically living
from hand to mouth when he visited Meredith Hall as a matter of
routine, to try to interest the school in his works. Silas must have had
the plan in mind for years. Everyone on the payroll has been destitute

at one time or another. But nonetheless they are all exceedingly able."

She gave a short laugh.

"The fact that the majority of them cannot ever be dismissed gives Silas the upper hand over Evangeline even after his death. He rules from the grave. And although Evangeline puts family above all else, she cannot forgive her father for that. The original staff was entirely of his own choosing, and she cannot dismiss them."

"And how about Eleanor Vaughn?"

She moved close to me and lowered her voice.

"Things are coming to a strange pass here. Since Eleanor's death there has been a change. There is a singularly morbid tension existing in the student body. Something has widened the breach within the faculty itself."

"How did Eleanor happen to secure a position here at all?"

"Through Silas. The art teacher left—Emmeline had introduced art classes in the curriculum, and Eleanor stepped into the position. She ingratiated herself very subtly into the old man's affections. He gave her a life long job and a surprisingly large sum of money from the estate. The money was to revert to Philip if she died first. The girl was very pretty and rather talented, but there was something strange there . . . In spite of that, Eleanor did her work satisfactorily."

I looked at my companion. Why had she tacked that last line on?

"And what about Mr. James and Eleanor Vaughn?"

"They were—well, practically engaged, you know. Eleanor's marriage to Philip would have made her really secure. The will left the residue of the estate to Philip and the two girls, but if Philip marries, his wife will get one-quarter of the income from the school."

Suddenly she stopped as though she had gone far enough.

"Let us go back upstairs. The others may have returned by now. We'll go to our rooms by way of the front stairs. I want to see if Homer has come back. If he has, he may be in the library reading. He never thinks of going to our room unless I remind him that it's bedtime."

I followed her through the gloom, up out of the cold underground recesses.

We moved toward the front of the building, along the wide corridor that ran through the entire structure.

There was no one in the library, but as we came around a bend in the hall we saw a thin bar of gold under the door which led into Miss Evangeline's office.

To my surprise, my companion said nothing about the light. My eyes took in the hall closet. I recalled, in that instant, another mysterious adventure and on the spur of the moment asked, "Mrs. Fiske, could you tell me who is the owner of the green plaid umbrella that I see so often in the closet?"

"You mean the one with a lion's head for a handle?"

"Yes . . ."

We were moving up the staircase now. Far down below us the light still burned in Miss Evangeline's office.

"Why, that umbrella belongs to me," Cornelia Fiske said. "What about it?"

"Oh, nothing," I said feebly. "I borrowed it to go to class one rainy day. It's such an odd handle that I was curious to know who the owner was."

"People are always borrowing my umbrella," Cornelia Fiske said. "It would seem there are no others in the school."

She looked at me fixedly and added, "It is just one more evidence of lack of respect for another's property."

Then she ran up the steps and left me at my door with a curt good night. Later on, as I climbed into bed I tried to figure out what it all meant. I had the distinct feeling that Cornelia Fiske had been trying to trap me into something down in the Meredith family vault. As I fell asleep, I saw her eyes again. They almost seemed to be saying, "Perhaps this one will help . . ."

Chapter X

THE new term began uneventfully. And then Doctor Rudlow frightened me one day when he examined my throat. At that time there was a grippe epidemic, and it was usual to find the doctor's car parked in front of the Hall at almost any hour. I must confess that I had been puzzled when I discovered that the strange man I had seen in the black car with Miss Evangeline and Helena the night of Diana's escapade was the school physician. But I had thought no more about it.

It was just after he had thrown the tongue compressor into the wastebasket and was casually placing his instruments in his little black bag that he inquired casually, "Have you ever had a nervous breakdown, Miss Hunter?"

"No, Doctor, never."

"But you are high-strung, suffer from emotional exhaustion?"

"If you mean that I become easily excited over things, well, I do and I don't. I've always had more than my share of responsibility and had to keep very level-headed—"

"Just as I thought. And now the brain is a bit tired, is it not? Sometimes you do not sleep well—"

"That's true, but—"

"And I suppose you think everyone wishes to persecute you?"

This was a trap of some sort, and I was slipping into it.

"No, no," I cried.

"I am not going to harm you . . . Come, Miss Hunter, control your-self."

I looked into his eyes and saw that he was not interested in helping me. Fortunately someone knocked on the door. He became very professional and opened it. Miss Evangeline came into the room.

"I just wanted to see how you found our Miss Hunter, Dr. Rudlow. We must take every precaution in guarding against the spread of colds. Any teacher who has contracted one should not be permitted to mingle with the students."

"Her throat is not bad. A little red, perhaps, but frequent gargling will cause that to disappear. These capsules," he emptied a few from a white box onto my desk, "will drive the germ out of her system."

"Thank you. I will take one immediately."

He continued, "I think perhaps you are overworking Miss Hunter. She tells me she has difficulty in sleeping."

Before I could protest this distortion of my words, Miss Evangeline replied, "I'm sure that medicine you recommended for my sister should relieve Miss Hunter."

The doctor looked thoughtful.

"Perhaps you are right."

He wrote out a perscription and gave it to Miss Evangeline.

"Mrs. Hawkins is going to the village directly," she said amiably. "She will leave this at the pharmacy for you."

"Thank you," I said dully.

"I am happy to help you. Now rest . . . spend the day in bed."

"But I feel well! And the doctor says I may conduct my classes."

"I will see that Mrs. Hawkins has your lunch brought to you," she went on as though I had not said anything.

In the days that followed, Miss Evangeline was extremely affable toward me. But I felt that this affability cloaked some drastic plan, and I had no faith in Dr. Rudlow. His fees for both faculty and students were exorbitant, but it appeared to be an unwritten law that everyone had to use him. This seemed even stranger when I discovered that he ran a sanitarium some distance away and was not even a local man.

Miss Evangeline was most interested in my health. One day she asked me if I thought the pills had helped, and I was forced to reply untruthfully that I did. I hadn't the slightest idea whether they could help or not, for I had never used them. I went to my room and fished out the bottle of pills from beneath a pile of lingerie. Now I carefully figured out how many pills I would have used had I taken three a day. Then I dumped that number from the bottle and flung them down the drain. Aside from this, these winter days were my most tranquil at Meredith Hall.

It was Elaine who broke the thread of the existing peace. It all began with the arrival of a special delivery letter, and it ended in tragedy.

I was on the way to class when a messenger boy arrived with the letter. The parlormaid signed for it and hastened with it to Miss Evangeline's office. There did not appear to be anything portentous attached to that letter, and I immediately forgot about it.

My students were particularly lackadaisical that morning. It was with mutual relief that we saw the hour draw to a close, and I welcomed a free period before the next class.

For the first time in many weeks I sat down at a drafting table, pencil in hand, and began to sketch. I had always found sketching an antidote to boredom. I was working away absorbedly when I heard the door open.

"Who is it?" I called out, without turning around.

"Elaine."

Something about her voice made me wheel abruptly. A certain ethereal beauty clung to the child's thin, white countenance, but the eyes were deeply sunken and the cheek bones too pronounced. And all this had happened since I had first seen her.

"Come in. Take off your things and pull up a chair, I'm sketching you for my cousin, Julian. He can't wait until he sees you this summer. He's already planning our holiday."

"There won't be any holiday for me."

She flung herself upon a chair without removing her coat.

"My father's will has been probated . . . My father didn't—didn't die a rich man. It seems he owed a good deal of money, and certain investments went bad—"

"My dear child," I said, bewildered, "suppose your father did leave you less than you expected . . ."

"Don't you understand? It's not enough to keep me here but because my father bequeathed his books and antiques to Meredith Hall, Miss Evangeline's agreed to keep me on until my guardian returns—as—as some sort of—charity pupil."

"When did you hear about this?"

"You should have heard him, Miss Hunter. He was so grateful . . . *grateful,* to her, when I hate her so! Now I'm stuck. I'm a prisoner—"

And then she ran to me, buried her head in my lap, and sobbed her heart out. There had to be something I could do to help this child. But, deep in my heart, I knew there was nothing I could do.

In a muffled voice Elaine spoke again.

"And all those books and precious things that Mother bought. Why didn't he leave them to me? Why didn't he?"

"I don't know, dear. After all, he expected you to remain at Meredith

Hall, and probably he decided you would enjoy having those familiar things about you."

"Do you really think that's what he meant?" she asked, wanting desperately to believe me.

"Yes, and perhaps Miss Evangeline will let you hang one of your favorite paintings over your bed."

"Perhaps she will! There was one that Mother was terribly fond of."

We went outdoors for a while and walked along the cliff. The sea air, as Doctor Rudlow claimed, was bracing, and soon some color returned to Elaine's cheeks. I brought her back to the studio in a more cheerful frame of mind.

But my effort had been in vain, for not many days later, Miss Evangeline contrived to alter the child's status at the school. I arrived at lunch one day and found another girl sitting in Elaine's place.

"Where's Elaine?"

"Don't you know?" asked Eliza Horning. "She's been shifted to Mademoiselle's table."

That afternoon the usual Wednesday faculty meeting demanded my presence.

Philip was not there—he was the only one who dared to take such a liberty.

On this day, Elaine was the chief subject of discussion. Her lost income was dwelt upon at great length. Evangeline said that Elaine could not be dropped.

Why, I wondered, was dear Evangeline so willing to keep a pupil for whom she had little affection? What was behind her sudden benevolence?

"I agree with my sister," chimed in Helena. "It would be unfair to dismiss an old student so peremptorily."

Corneila Fiske demurred, "If this is not supposed to be a charity school, would we not be setting a dangerous precedent?"

Our Headmistress glowered at this, then she replied calmly, "Of course we have no wish to sacrifice a penny of our hard-earned money, but that won't be necessary. Elaine's tuition has been paid through March. Whatever allowance she receives, in the future, from Mr. Morgan—who will be in Shanghai these next two years—I will apply against any expenses that may accrue on her behalf. Meanwhile she will have to sacrifice pleasures and privileges enjoyed by the other girls, unless she cares to earn the extra money."

In a moment, I though, I shall know why Elaine is being kept on.

"Only last week," the Headmistress said, "one of you mentioned the fact that Miss Perkins needs an assistant. Now who did bring that up?"

"It was Philip, considerate boy," said Mundin. "I remember how he deplored the way we overworked the woman."

"Philip! So the idea originated with Philip—" Miss Evangeline murmured half to herself, and then added more forcefully, "I thought it might be a good idea for Elaine to help Miss Perkins."

"Good old Evangeline," George beamed, "I knew you'd find a way out. I can always trust you to see that I hold on to my fortune as long as it is tied up with yours!"

Miss Evangeline showed her disapproval. "George, you forget yourself!"

"But to help the seamstress," I found myself exclaiming, "that doesn't seem fair. The other students will look down upon Elaine. Children can't help being unkind." I paused for an instant. "Elaine hates sewing."

"Those girls who look down upon her will be severely punished," Miss Evangeline replied angrily.

I realized then that I was blundering, but a look of sympathy from Mademoiselle encouraged me to go on.

"Don't you see," I begged the group, "Elaine loves her art work. She's really gifted. If she has to help Miss Perkins she will have no free time for herself. The girls will soon form the habit of turning small tasks over to her, and—"

"Why shouldn't they? How do I know but what the child will be left a complete pauper, and then we'll have her on our hands. At least let us have her learn something useful. I'm afraid art won't help her if she is left to earn her own living. You must know, only too well, the difficulties in finding work in that field. It will be far better for her to take extra courses under Miss Valentine, and to have less art. I will see that she is transferred from most of her classes."

Once again while trying to help Elaine I had managed to involve her in further difficulty.

Miss Evangeline's final decision seemed to meet with the unanimous approval of my colleagues. No further objections were offered.

"You wanted to question the teachers about Diana Marden," prompted Helena.

"Ah, yes," said Miss Evangeline, but she seemed annoyed at the reminder. "I'm sure that there are no complaints. Diana is one of our representative students."

"She has a tricky way of slipping out of the dormitory," said Henrietta with a coy nod of her head. "She deceived me two weeks ago."

"And paid for her error," retorted Miss Evangeline.

"By the way," drawled George Mundin, "that fund must be growing by leaps and bounds, what?"

"I don't understand your insinuation, George. If you are referring to the School Fund, let me remind you of the expense involved in equipping the gymnasium with three new enclosed showers this year."

Diana's clique immediately assumed the attitude which I had foreseen. I often felt that these girls deliberately ripped buttons from their clothes in order to give Elaine something to do. Certainly, the sewing room had never been more popular.

Once I overheard Diana offer Elaine money. It must have been a bribe, for I heard Diana say, "Go on, do it for me. I'll pay you lots, and you can thumb your nose at Evangeline."

I had been on my way to the dormitory when this occurred, for since Elaine had been banned from her art courses I forfeited much of my free time to give her private lessons.

I did not make my presence known, for here was a chance to get to the bottom of the mystery of Diana's escapades.

"I'm sorry, Diana," Elaine said, "I couldn't do anything like that."

"Very well," said Diana nastily, "be a servant. That's what Evangeline intends to make you. Just wait and see!"

She flounced out of the dormitory.

When I came into the room, Elaine was staring out of the window. Why couldn't I leave Meredith Hall, I thought, just go away, give up, forget? I looked at Elaine, and I knew one reason why I couldn't go. And Julian was another reason, and there was a third—Philip. I helped Elaine on with her coat, and we set out for the studio.

It was Saturday afternoon. Almost all of the students had gone to town or the city. But as we went down the stairs I heard the even rat-tat of a typewriter. It came from the half-open door of Philip's office.

As we reached the ground floor, the typing unexpectedly ceased. The door was flung open, and Philip stalked into the hall.

He laughed and asked what we were up to.

"Miss Hunter is going to give me an art lesson," Elaine said.

"Isn't that carrying things a bit too far? Surely Elaine hasn't been so wayward that she needs to forfeit a Saturday outing to make up her art work."

I hesitated. If I explained, it would look as though I were carrying tales, looking for sympathy. Before I reached a decision Elaine told the whole story.

"It does seem a bit drastic to have to give up all art classes," Philip said.

"Oh, I still have my lecture course, but Miss Evangeline thought it was more practical for me to devote myself to the domestic sciences."

"Well, Miss Evangeline may be right, you know," he said with a pleasant and rare smile. "But don't study too hard now. After all, it is Saturday."

The afternoon passed pleasantly. Elaine worked industriously. She was going a water color of a cat, and Boots, content and warm, was a willing subject. Meanwhile I put the finishing touches to the pastel of Elaine which I had made from the rough pencil sketch sent to Julian. The likeness was very good.

"Oh," she exclaimed, "I'm not as pretty as that."

"Prettier. If those cheeks of yours would only fill out."

I stood the finished portrait on the mantelpiece. Then I suggested that we go for a walk.

Instead of taking the usual path which led back to the driveway, we struck across the grounds, the snow crackling cheerfully beneath our heavy galoshes.

We walked along in silence, listening to the crunch-crunch of our boots on the ground. Dusk was gradually deepening into dark evening, and Elaine began to peer about timidly when suddenly, as we rounded a thick cluster of trees, we saw Philip coming toward us.

At first he was not aware of us, for he was lost in thought. When he saw us he looked startled, as if we had caught him doing something he wanted kept a secret. And then he seemed angry.

"O-oh, let's go back with Mr. James," pleaded Elaine, as, after a brief and formal interchange of words, I was about to continue.

It was growing dark rapidly, but I most certainly did not wish to force my company on anyone as ungracious as Philip James.

"Please let's," begged Elaine.

"Come along," said Philip impatiently. "There's no point in loitering here and freezing to death."

I longed to answer angrily that it wasn't I who had suggested joining him, but what was the use?

"Let's go," I said.

When we reached the Hall, with a brief, "Good night," Philip went away. No sooner had his footfalls been absorbed by the carpet in the main corridor than Helena stood before us.

"So," she said, "you have finally returned. I trust you enjoyed your walk. Now I understand why you were so eager to tutor Elaine private-ly. You use the child as a cover for your own—shall we say illicit—carryings on?"

Elaine clung to me. I stared at Helena in amazement.

Her eyes dilated horribly. She looked for the first time like her portrait in the Seahouse. There was a pinched look about her nostrils, heavy black circles under her eyes, and her skin was ghastly white. Fine veins stood out in her thin throat.

"Go to your room, Elaine," she commanded.

"Why? What have I done?"

"Don't question me," Helena screamed. "You are to do as you are told. Report to Miss Evangeline after supper."

Reluctantly Elaine left us alone.

Helena turned on me.

"I saw you follow him into the woods, and it's not the first time you've been there either."

"Whatever do you mean?"

"So—Well, let me enlighten you. I saw you cross the lawn with Elaine. As soon as you saw Mr. James turn into the woods, you followed him."

"Oh, no! That's not true. I—"

"I must take action to see that Elaine is protected. From now on you will keep away from her. We do not think you are a fit companion for Elaine."

"You can't mean that. Why she looks forward to her lessons. She—"

Helena turned and left me alone in the hall.

For a long time I stood there, allowing the full meaning of her insinuations to sink in. Then wearily I picked up my wet galoshes and tucked them under my arm. Just as I reached the foyer I saw Elaine rush out of Miss Evangeline's office. I called to her, and I knew she must have heard me, but she did not stop. Helena had lost no time.

Whatever the Headmistress told Elaine certainly convinced the child that she must avoid me. I rarely saw her, since she only attended one art lecture each week, for she always managed to come to class just when I was calling the roll, and she was among the first to leave when the hour was done.

Once, when I tried to detain her, I saw her glance nervously at Diana, and then she rushed from the studio. Another time I met her on the second floor of the Hall just as I came out of my room. Since we seemed to be alone, I stopped to speak to her.

"Elaine, my dear," I began a trifle awkwardly, "how are you?"

"I'm all right," she cut me off hastily, her lips quivering. "Please, Miss Hunter, it's dangerous for us to be seen together."

"Why? Tell me."

Before she could reply, we heard voices coming from the main hall, and she rushed away.

That was the last attempt I made to speak privately to Elaine until the morning a letter arrived from Julian. The first part was for me, but the rest was intended for Elaine. In his humorous fashion he had written to Elaine that, upon receipt of the drawing I had made of her, he had immediately fallen in love with the subject and would that subject please write to him?

What to do about the letter was a problem. The letter had to be answered, and by Elaine herself, or Julian would be hurt.

I sat down at the desk in my room and penned a brief note to Elaine. The note written, I sent for Mary.

I explained what I wished her to do, and then the envelope was transferred to the pocket of her apron.

"I'll find Miss Elaine and see that this is safely delivered. Don't you be worryin' about it any more."

"Do be sure that no one sees you give it to her."

"Leave it to Mary. This afternoon Miss Perkins is comin'. About four o'clock I'll be bringin' up her tea. Miss Elaine is always there at the time. Now, Miss Perkins always goes to wash her hands before she drinks the tea. She has to go out of the room to wash her hands—that's when I'll do it!"

She brushed aside my expressions of gratitude, and I saw her go, feeling lighterhearted than I had in many days. But late that afternoon a terrified Mary plunged me into despair.

"I found Miss Elaine alone in the sewin' room. She was so glad to get your letter. She grabbed it and tucked it away in the top of her stockin' to read later. Then she asked would I take the answer back to you and she'd leave it under the pillow of her bed after breakfast tomorrow."

But then as Mary had left the sewing room, she had seen a tall, brown-clad figure gliding noiselessly down the passageway.

Miss Evangeline's failure to announce her presence and the secrecy attending her departure were utterly terrifying. Surely she had heard the conversation. And now what were we to do?

At supper, however, our Headmistress greeted me with affability. This was worse than if she had abused me. But all that evening she was kindness itself.

The next morning when Elaine reported for class I caught her eye for a moment as she hung away her coat. I could see there was something she had to tell me, and in order not to draw too much attention to us, I pretended to adjust one of the bulbs in the floor lamp by the clothes rack.

"Did you get my answer?" she whispered as soon as I was close enough.

There were questions I wanted to ask, but all I could do was shake my head. Elaine sucked in her breath with a rasping sound and her coat slipped from her fingers. Mechanically I stooped to pick it up. The studio door opened and Miss Evangeline walked in.

"I hope you do not mind, Miss Hunter," she said, in a cordial, yet businesslike manner, "but I would like to observe your class this morning."

"Certainly, Miss Evangeline," I managed, "we are pleased to have you with us."

Diana Marden snickered. I tried to keep my voice calm while I discussed phases of art during the Italian Renaissance.

Miss Evangeline was superb. She sat there to one side of me, her hands folded gracefully in her lap.

When the hour ended, I expected Miss Evangeline to linger after the students had departed. Instead, she slowly and majestically got into her rich-looking seal coat and followed the girls from the studio.

By the end of the afternoon a blizzard let loose in all its devastating fury. Coming back to the main building from the studio at dusk, I was almost blinded by the heavy snowfall.

There was an ominous quiet about the building, and I tried to shake off a feeling that something was wrong. When I went down to supper I found Diana Marden and her followers waiting.

"Have you heard," Diana cried, "Elaine's run away!"

"No, no . . ." I murmured in shocked surprise.

"Oh, yes, it's true all right. She took her toothbrush, her nightclothes, and two dresses. Think of that little mouse having such nerve!" she laughed. "Hell will break loose when they find her."

"If they find her alive in this storm," put in Marjorie Jonas.

"She must have left around two o'clock," offered Eliza Horning, "because I was with her in the dorm till then. In fact, I was late for Latin because of Elaine. You see, she was upset, and—" the girl flushed uncomfortably, "I had been trying to cheer her up."

Somehow I knew that Eliza, at least, was no longer my enemy, but there wasn't time for such thoughts now.

"Did anyone see her leave?"

"No. Nobody seems to have seen her after Eliza."

"Did she say anything to you, Eliza, drop a hint?"

"No, I thought she seemed strange. Her eyes looked so bright, and her face was so flushed. I thought she had a fever."

"If she left after two o'clock she might have been overtaken by the storm before she reached town!" I exclaimed.

"They notified the village station and the bus terminal," said Edith Fenton. "An alarm has been sent out through the village, but they've had no word. It's such an awful storm!"

I couldn't bear inaction any longer. I flung my napkin down on the table, jumped up from my seat, and hurried down the dining room to where Miss Evangeline was calmly eating her food.

"Miss Evangeline!" I said loudly, "the girls have just told me about Elaine. Have you heard anything? What are you doing to find her?"

"We have notified all the authorities—"

"Yes, yes, I know all about that, but that's not enough! There should be a searching party—"

"Bravo!" said Mundin, applauding, "spoken like a Meredith!"

Just then Philip strode into the dining room. His clothes were encrusted with sleet.

"We've looked all over the grounds, Evangeline," he said. "There's not a sign of her. Johnson claims she did not pass through the gate, and he's been—"

"It was hardly necessary for you to go along, Philip. I'm sure that Johnson and Bill are quite capable."

"It takes more than three people to search the grounds," Philip said. "I've a few volunteers from the village who rode up on Jeggy Williams' sleigh. They're still out. I can't understand it. Johnson insists Elaine did not pass through the gate, and he was there until the storm began. She must be somewhere on the grounds."

"Suppose she left after the storm began," I said.

Philip looked at me, and I thought for an instant that his eyes softened. "The townspeople are picking up the search outside the grounds. They will be sure to find her if she's on the road."

"If—only if. She may have lost her way and be somewhere out in the fields. She still may be here—near the school."

"Don't worry," he said kindly, "every inch of space is being covered. We'll keep searching until we find her."

"This scandal won't help the school any," George Mundin said. "I should say you were a bit hasty in calling in the townspeople, what?"

"I'm a human being, Mundin."

"Of course," said Cornelia Fiske, "I'm in favor of doing all we can for the child, but it was a thoughtless act on her part."

Helena had been listening attentively. "Yes, after all we've done for her, too. Keeping her on when she couldn't even pay—"

"That's not so."

It was the first time I had heard Philip take a stand against the Merediths.

"Elaine's tuition is paid up through March," he went on. "All this talk about her being dependent on us is tommyrot. Mr. Morgan just sent in another check to cover her additional expenses. Why do we waste time talking? We should be out searching for the child. I'm ready now. Do any of you want to join me—Mundin? Homer? Geoff?"

Carter got to his feet. As Fiske moved to follow, Cornelia detained him.

"Homer, you can't go. You're not strong enough to go out in this weather."

He sank back into his seat.

Mundin toyed with a fork, raking the bread crumbs.

The next hour was a nightmare. The storm continued and no word was heard from the searching party. Students and faculty crowded the foyer and study hall waiting for news. Miss Evangeline kept to her office.

At nine o'clock the girls were sent off to bed. Then at last Philip came stamping in.

"We haven't found her yet, but we will. We need your help. I thought you might give us some clue. Is there any possible hideout where she might have gone?"

"The woods! The woods where we met you the other day."

"Good God, we'll never find that path. But—"

He swung on his heel and left us alone once more. Soon the other members of the faculty drifted away. Some even went to bed, and I was alone in the great, gloomy hall. I paced back and forth, to and fro, back and forth . . . And an eternity later, they brought Elaine in. She was blue with cold and half frozen. Philip had found her in a snowdrift in the woods, almost a mile from the school.

They carried her to a vacant room on the second floor. Mary helped me undress her, and Doctor Rudlow was sent for. By and by, she weakly fluttered her eyelids and said to me hoarsely, "I—tried to—get—away. If—it hadn't—snowed—I might—have."

"Yes, dear, I know, but now you mustn't talk. Just rest."

I stood in a shadowy corner as Doctor Rudlow came in with Helena and Miss Evangeline.

The physician subjected the girl to an examination which would have taxed the strength of a hardier soul and it left Elaine utterly exhausted. He was extremely grave. All three moved into the corridor. I caught a few of the words as he was saying.

"Pleurisy—one hundred and five—very sick—may develop into pneumonia—bears watching—I doubt she'll live through the night."

I came out of the shadows.

"Let me look after her. . . ."

"I hardly think you a suitable person to be charged with care of the patient, Miss Hunter," said Miss Evangeline. "Mrs. Hawkins is a practical nurse. She will take complete charge of the patient. You may visit Elaine during the day if Doctor Rudlow does not think your presence will excite her too much."

By the next morning Elaine had developed pneumonia. Doctor Rudlow's prediction had been right, and her temperature skyrocketed.

I could not bring myself to conduct a class and posted a notice on the bulletin board announcing that all art classes would be suspended for the day.

I kept a solitary vigil in the damp corridor outside of Elaine's room. At last the door opened and the physician emerged.

"All we can do now is ease her suffering," he said. "She is asking for you." He looked at Miss Evangeline for confirmation. "Perhaps if you remain at her bedside, it will soften her departure when it comes."

I do not know how I replied or what I did. I was still standing there, where they left me, when Miss Evangeline returned after seeing him out.

Finally I went in to sit with Elaine. A heavy, anesthetic odor permeated the air. Elaine lay with eyelids closed. In the anteroom I could hear Evangeline, Helena, and Mrs. Hawkins making plans for the funeral. I sat at Elaine's bedside, and I knew that Evangeline had done this—that Evangeline had contrived to have Elaine run away. But why? Why?

Some of the faculty members drifted in during the long hours. No one stayed for very long, and I was grateful when I was left alone. Late that evening Elaine opened her eyes.

"Miss Hunter . . ."

"Yes, dear?"

"Are—we—alone?"

"Yes, we are."

"I know I'm going to die. That's—why—it's so important I tell—you —now. Remember you asked me about—the last time—I saw Eleanor Vaughn—"

"Yes."

She did not go on and without turning around I knew.

Miss Evangeline was there. She was approaching the bed.

"Go away, go away," sobbed Elaine, attempting to raise herself from the pillow.

Evangeline moved to the foot of the bed.

With a supreme effort Elaine raised herself from the pillow, and pointing at Miss Evangeline screamed, "Be careful—of her. Go away from here, Miss Hunter."

Suddenly her eyes grew round with amazement and then she lay there, very still, glaring up out of large, glassy blue eyes . . .

Chapter XI

I⸱T SEEMED hours later that I was tearing down the front stairs sobbing hysterically. I did not even see Philip in the great hall as I rushed out into the night. I ran beneath icy boughs. I ran and I wept. I plunged off the path through a bordering clump of trees and thickets. They tore at me, but I was determined to get away where I could be alone with my grief.

"Steady."

It was a man's voice.

"You'll take terrific punishment if you force your way through there."

I turned. Philip stood there in the moonlight. I let him guide me back to the driveway. He held my arm, and his clasp was strong and comforting. It seemed the most natural thing in the world to have him walking by my side, handing me a big handkerchief to wipe my eyes.

"So it's all over," he said ever so gently.

I nodded speechlessly as we continued to trudge through huge drifts, past the studio and along the cliff. After a time, he spoke again.

"You were very fond of her, weren't you?"

"I loved her. I wanted so to make her happy, but I couldn't. She was afraid—to the very end."

"Afraid of what?"

"She never had the chance to tell me."

"Why, you're shivering!" he exclaimed in concern. "I'm going to take you right back to the Hall before you catch cold yourself."

"No, no. I don't want to go back to that awful place. Not ever."

"You mustn't speak that way," he said softly. "I know you're too sensible to give in to your emotions."

"I have no one to go back to now. I've lost the only friend I had there."

"No," he said unexpectedly, taking my cold hand in his and rubbing it gently, "you aren't alone. You have another friend."

He clasped my hand.

We stood gazing down at the sea. The waves lashed the jagged precipice. I would have remained there with him forever, but he drew me gently away from the cliff, back toward the school.

At the front door, he said, "You mustn't be afraid of Meredith Hall. I used to be when I first came here to live as a boy. And remember," he added, "if there is anything you need, even if it's just a shoulder to —weep on, I'll be there."

"Thank you," I whispered, "oh, thank you."

Elaine's funeral service was held in the school chapel. Nothing was omitted from the ceremony which could possibly be included. The heavy chanting of lamentation, the wailing of the organ music, all proclaimed a time of mourning.

Philip summoned me to his office as soon as we left the chapel. He looked at me more sternly than he had ever done.

"Sit down, Miss Hunter," he commanded.

He cleared his throat. Then he crossed to the window and stared out through the curtains, his back to me.

"It's unhealthy to mope and mourn," he said gruffly. "One's thoughts must not linger forever with the dead . . . I know."

Suddenly he swung about.

"You and I must help each other to forget, do you see?"

I sat there woodenly.

"You probably don't see . . ."

He paced restlessly to and fro.

"The pall of someone else's death has been hanging over me for months now. It's consuming my mind and body to such a degree that sometimes I also feel I can't go on. 'Work,' they say, 'work will bring you salvation,' but I say work is not enough!"

He faced me once more.

"If we live only for work, we are but half human. There are other things in life," he said fiercely. "Come here," he commanded.

I went to him.

He stared at me in silence. Then he took a swift step toward me, and I was in his arms. He kissed my lips, my eyes, my throat, and then my lips again. These were hard, scorching kisses, without tenderness or love. Suddenly he released me.

"Forgive me," he said. "Forgive me. I don't want you to love me. I'm not asking you to love me. I'm just asking for your friendship . . . That's what I want. That's what I need."

"Very well," I said, trying to sound as though my heart were not breaking, trying to sound as though I did not want to kiss his mouth, now, at once, forever, "it's a pact. We're going to help each other forget."

We kept to our pact and tried desperately not to dwell in the past. For me it was easier. I had no self-torment. I had done my best for Elaine. And as the days passed, I could not help but feel she was happier where she was.

One Saturday afternoon, a short time later, I was out on the cliff sketching. It was one of those rare winter days when there is a hint of spring.

For a long time I had been anxious to put on canvas the savage ocean beating against the jagged rocks at the foot of the precipice. As was usual when I was alone, my thoughts were of Philip.

And, when I thought about Philip, Eleanor Vaughn was never far off. I looked involuntarily at the rocks below. I was assembling my drawing paraphernalia, having decided not to draw any more, when I felt that someone was watching me. I looked up and found Helena Meredith staring at me. Unkempt hair hung over her forehead and face, and mud clung to her boots and stockings. The collar of her blouse hung over the coat. A dirty petticoat protruded from beneath the skirt.

"I have been watching you work for some time," she said.

"I intend to paint the scene at the foot of the cliff," I explained. "It's beautiful in a primitive way."

"Yes."

She went to the elge of the cliff and peered over.

"Look," she said, beckoning me to her side. "That is where Eleanor lay."

She took my arm and pointed to a spot where the rocks had formed a shelf against the side of a cliff.

"Her titian hair was spreading a halo about her head. Only when you came closer could you tell it was matted with blood. Her hat had rolled away. We found it right by the water. One shoe had disappeared.

It may be buried somewhere in the sand below. Why couldn't they have found the shoe?"

She released my arm. I moved hastily away. When she finally came back to where I stood, the half-mad light had faded from her face, and she looked dull and mousey once more. I accepted her offer to assist me, and we carried my equipment back to the studio.

"Are you happy here at the school?"

"I'm content with my work."

"The teachers take what the Hall can give them, but no one gives anything in return."

"I wouldn't say that. We give our services. Certainly you and Miss Evangeline and Philip—" I caught myself too late.

"You speak of Mr. James as though you were familiar with his contribution to the school," she said with a nonchalance I mistrusted. Her body had grown tense.

"I've read a few of his pamphlets and found them very good. He even let me look over part of his thesis. I think," I said carefully, "Mr. James is going to prove himself worthy of the confidence your father had in him."

By this time we were inside the studio, and I moved toward the east room.

Helena did not seem to hear me, for her eyes were darting curiously about until they finally rested on my portrait of Elaine.

"Who made this?"

"I did. Do you like it?"

"Very much."

The unexpected appearance of Boots broke in on this very affable exchange. I had not noticed the cat creep into the room, but at the sight of Helena, she wailed dolefully. Helena seized an andiron and went after Boots. I grasped her hand.

"Don't hurt her, Miss Helena. I'll let her out."

I opened the cottage door and shooed poor Boots away.

Helena shouted, "Get rid of that cat. I never want to see her again, do you hear?"

"I'll get rid of her as soon as possible," I assured Helena. "Just as soon as I find another home for her."

With a feeling of relief I watched her return the andiron to its customary place. I buttoned my coat and pulled my worn pigskin gloves from my pocket. I didn't care for Helena's company, and I left as soon as I could.

I had intended to cut across the grounds to the ridge, but the snow had turned to slush, and it was not pleasant underfoot. I paused to tighten a loosened zipper on my galoshes, and after a brief delay, walked along the gravel path toward the main drive. I felt that I was being followed. Innumerable times I turned my head, but I saw no one. At the intersection of the path and driveway, I heard a loud toot of a horn and looking up, caught sight of a familiar dark blue roadster.

"Philip," I cried, waving my hand eagerly.

"Hop in. I'm on my way to the post office to mail part of my thesis to the printers."

In a few seconds we were spinning through the gate and down toward the town.

"How about our stopping for a hot chocolate?" suggested Philip.

Soon we were giving our orders to the drugstore proprietor, and then Philip removed his manuscript from the folder. "It's a pretty long-winded affair."

"It has to be. One could write volumes on 'The Psychological in Shakespeare.'"

"This is just a prelude to future work. I wonder," he said, suddenly growing moody, "whether I'm on the right track or not. There's so much I want to accomplish. I want time for writing and lectures, yet I don't like to give up my teaching. It wouldn't be fair to Silas."

"Tell me something about Silas Meredith. What was he like?"

"Well, he was a difficult person to know. He was all mind, and he was hard. Some even found him cruel, but he was very generous to me, particularly after my mother died."

"How long ago did she die?" I asked.

"About ten years ago. She was thrown from a horse."

"How shocking!"

"It was a shock. She was such a good rider. The horse just lost its head. Evangeline was there when the accident happened. She had to break the news to everyone. She hasn't been on a horse since."

I felt a sudden pounding in my head. Evangeline and death. Evangeline and death. Somehow I couldn't disconnect the two. And then I was fearful, abjectly fearful for Philip and for myself.

"Philip," I asked impulsively, "does working here at the Hall entirely satisfy you?"

"What a strange question. I never could leave the Hall completely. Not that the building holds any enchantment for me, but I'm bound by other ties. I may leave it for a few months to lecture elsewhere, but it's been my world for so long that I could never break with it altogether. It's hard to explain, though there are important financial reasons, too, but I am a part of Meredith Hall."

He got up abruptly and we left the drugstore. We crossed the street to the post office. Philip mailed his manuscript, and while he was doing so I remembered Boots.

"Do you know anything about sending a cat?" I asked one of the attendants.

He scratched his head in bewilderment. "Don't believe anyone ever asked me that before." He called across to the man who was taking care of Philip. "Say, Pete, here's a question for you?"

"Tell it to the Professor," said the other clerk with a grin.

"What's that?" asked Philip.

"How to send a cat," I explained. "Miss Helena insists I dispose of Eleanor Vaughn's—"

"Lan's sakes," broke in the first clerk. "Good thing you mentioned that name. There's a letter I've been holding here. It came for Miss Vaughn a few days ago. I said to Pete, 'That woman's dead, what will we do about it?' Pete there said, 'Guess the message can't be very important if the writer waits until the woman's dead.' It was mailed here in town. Do you want to open it, Mr. James?"

"No," Philip said quietly. "Return it."

My attempts at conversation as we drove back to the Hall failed to awaken any response. It was quite obvious that Philp was far away.

"This letter," I began, sending out a tiny feeler, "was written by someone quite recently. Why do you suppose that person wasn't notified about the accident?"

"I don't know, Evangeline took care of the notices."

"Don't you think that it would have been kinder to get in touch with whomever it was, and explain your reason for having the letter returned?"

He turned on me furiously.

"Why do you persist in this senseless questioning?"

"It isn't senseless, it's—I wish I knew what she could no longer face!"

"Nancy, please—I beg of you."

"Let me out here, Philip."

We had reached the studio path.

"You're running away."

"No, Philip. I feel like going to the sea-house for a while to think things through."

I was out of the car and hurrying along the path. I was free to sob and cry. There was no one to witness my unhappiness. But the tears refused to come.

I admitted myself to the studio. A light left carelessly burning in the east room drew my attention. It looked like a deliberate gesture made by Helena to involve me in difficulties with her sister.

I passed through the doorway and gasped. Standing on the mantelpiece, completely obscuring the painting of Elaine, was the strange sketch I had first noticed on the night of my arrival.

"I'm sorry to have startled you," said the subject of the painting, gliding softly into the room. "But of course I should have known better." This was a new Helena, kind, solicitous. I did not know whether the change was welcome.

"You are certainly free to come and go as you please," I said, and then, "after all, you have a key of your own."

"I've been looking over my portrait. You know Eleanor began it. Do you think you could finish it for me?"

"Why, I—you flatter me, Miss Helena. I'm not sure I'm capable of pleasing you."

"On the contrary, I'm sure you can do it even better than Eleanor, and that is high praise. The picture you did of Elaine is sufficient recommendation for me." She turned back toward the drawing, and spoke dreamily, "Out on the cliff, with the ocean as a background, just as dear Eleanor was doing it."

Then, as though the vision were ended, she rose to her feet, straightened her coat and smiled upon me brightly.

"I want the picture to hang in the gallery, the family gallery."

Chapter XII

DURING THE days that followed, Helena kept after me to work on the portrait. I spent many a late afternoon with Helena, working in the west room.

It was on one of these occasions about a week later that Philip stopped in at the studio.

Helena caught sight of him first.

"Philip," she exclaimed eagerly. "I'm glad that you called for me."

"Why, Helena, what made you ever have that idea?"

"Then what was your reason for coming?"

"I came to see Miss Hunter." He spoke to me, then. "Would you care to go to the Ice Carnival with me?"

He stood there as if it were an ordeal, and for a moment I didn't know what to say. I did so want to go with him, but Helena was staring at me, and I hesitated.

"Well, Miss Hunter," Philip said curtly, "what about it, will you go? It's this coming Saturday, you know."

I found my voice at last. "Thank you, Mr. James. If there is no need for my staying at the Hall, I shall enjoy going. I'll have to get my skates sharpened," I added enthusiastically. "They're frightfully dull."

"I'm riding into the village this evening. I'll take them to be sharpened, so they'll be ready for Saturday."

Then he went away.

"Shall we continue, Miss Helena?" I asked. I was being a cat and enjoying it.

Helena moved back upon the throne into her former position. She remained silent, but her eyes burned fiercely. I tried to return to work, but found that I could only make a few unimportant strokes. My hand was too shaky, and I certainly was not in the mood. I looked at Helena. Her throat was working furiously and her eyes were filled with black hate. I stopped working altogether. Helena seemed just as pleased to stop, and she ran out of the studio immediately, muttering to herself.

That night while I was going over student drawings at my desk, Mary came into my room. She was all excitement.

"Oh, Miss Hunter, Mr. James has really asked you to the Carnival. The fun you'll be a-havin'!" Then, as if a thought flashed through her mind to disturb her enthusiasm, she spoke more earnestly. "And it will be trouble that you'll be havin', too." She shrugged. "But you are a true daughter of Ireland. At least enough to take care of yourself."

"What do you mean, Mary?"

"There might be plenty of trouble comin' from what I overheard this evening, just after supper. I happened to be downstairs and went by Mr. James' office. Miss Evangeline was in there. I could hear Miss Evangeline askin' Mr. James if the two of them were going to the Carnival together. He up and says he's already invited you."

I could see that Mary was going to omit something so I said, "What else was there, Mary?"

"Well, nothing much, only then Miss Evangeline says, sweetly, 'It must be pleasant to be such a very eligible bachelor as you are, Philip, what with money, the school and all—' "

Saturday was a beautiful day. It was just cold enough to be invigorating. Even before lunch, a large gathering had assembled in the stands along the lake. I saw to it that the excited girls found places in the bus as it made many trips back and forth to the school. And after the last busload had been sent on its way, Philip met me at the door with a cutter, and I climbed in. Evangeline had gone with the last bus and the school was practically deserted. Only a few of the students, I found out, were not well enough to attend, and these were taken care of by some of the servants.

The iceboat races were over when we arrived at the lake. Crowds of skaters were gliding up and down, and those in charge of the affair were putting up ropes for the races. In the center of the roped area were to be the fancy exhibitions. Some of the racers were trying out the track. Philip and I put on our skates, then moved up the lake. The clink of the metal on the smooth hard ice was wonderful. After we had become used to each other's steps, we went in for more intricate formations.

"Why, you're good!" he exclaimed.

As Philip and I passed the grandstand, I caught a glimpse of Evangeline and Helena watching us. Their faces were inscrutable.

Once we saw Henrietta Valentine with George Mundin. They were at a table in the clubhouse and there seemed to be some trouble between them. But I would not let other people and their lives bother me. Not today.

The Carnival lasted until about ten in the evening and the climax was to be a beautiful display of fireworks. Music blared from the loudspeakers set up on the outside of the clubhouse. Couples glided rhythmically to the music. The lights, the gaiety, the glittering steel were utterly exhilarating.

"Let's get away from here," Philip suggested. "Let's go to the roadside inn at the bend in the lake. It's only a few miles from here. They serve a wonderful dinner and we can see the fireworks from there. We can dance, too. Do you dance as well as you waltz on skates?"

"What about the others?" In my mind were the faces of the Meredith sisters. "Do you think that it will be all right?"

"Why, of course. This is a holiday. It's Saturday night, and there's no curfew for us."

We left the inn late, wonderfully late, and Philip headed the horses toward the school. It was a glorious night. The moon was a big yellow ball as we made our way up the hill.

Then Philip looked at me, and he put an arm around my shoulder. "It is beautiful, isn't it?"

His lips almost brushed mine. Then he pulled himself away; he flicked the whip, and lapsed into one of his moody silences as the cutter sped forward.

We were at the Hall now. One of the servants had waited up, and he took the sleigh from the entrance. Philip and I went into the house. As we entered the front hall, a faint rustle made us both glance in the direction of the library. There, standing silently in the doorway, was Miss Evangeline.

"I thought it might be you, Philip," she said after a long pause. "I was worried about your being out so late."

She moved forward and toward him, ignoring me completely.

Philip looked uncomfortable.

"It was hardly necessary, Evangeline. Everything is all right. We stayed at the inn longer than we intended."

She waited a moment and said, "I'm glad you were able to enjoy yourself, Philip, dear. After all—" she continued pointedly, "it is such a short time since Eleanor passed away."

"Oh, God—Evangeline, please!"

She knew his vulnerable spot. I could have choked her.

After a long time, Philip said quietly—too quietly, "You're right,

Evangeline, but—" his voice was edged, "but you seem to forget that it is only human to crave some happiness in life!"

"You are quite right, Philip, but—" she drew herself up, "—since you blame yourself for Eleanor Vaughn's death—"

It was a ghastly moment. Then Philip turned and started up the stairs.

"Philip, Philip . . ."

Evangeline moved quickly after him. This was obviously not according to her plan.

"Philip," she repeated beseechingly, "forgive me. I did not realize what I was saying."

Philip turned and looked down. He looked lost and unhappy.

"Forgive me, Philip," Evangeline said again. "I'm tired. Sometimes all this responsibility is too much. It is so easy to speak too hastily."

Philip descended and clasped Evangeline's outstretched hand.

"I guess we are both tired, Evangeline."

Then Philip turned and came to me.

"Good night," he said. "You see—what happened today was all a mistake." In a voice meant for my ears alone, with eyes that looked deeply into mine, he said, "Now you know—there can be no hope for me." Then he went up the stairs once more.

Evangeline stood looking at me and upon her face there was a triumphant smile.

Chapter XIII

IN THE days after the Carnival, I could not shut out the memory of Evangeline's words to Philip. Evangeline's voice followed me from bedroom to seahouse, from dining hall to library. "You blame yourself for her death . . . you blame yourself for her death." At night I sank into sleep with the words ringing in my ears, and in the morning I awoke to the sound of those awful words.

Although I considered them from every angle, I could not fathom their meaning. All I knew was that by these words Evangeline had separated us. The breach was wider than it had ever been before Elaine's death.

The longer I worked for Evangeline Meredith the more I grew to fear her cunning. I tried to understand what motivated her. Perhaps it would upset her plans to have Philip take a wife. Perhaps that's what it was all really about.

Evangeline met no one on an equal footing save Doctor Rudlow. They were close friends. And how close I only realized after I had been at the Hall several months.

One afternoon I had just gone to my room, when there was a knock at the door.

"Telephone for you, Miss Hunter," one of the chambermaids told me as I opened the door.

"Telephone for me? Are you sure?"

"Yes, Miss Hunter. Miss Evangeline herself took the call. She says you may use the extension in her room."

The maid conducted me to the stately, luxurious chamber occupied by the Headmistress.

"Right here, Miss Hunter."

The girl indicated the telephone on the marble-topped night table and then left me alone. Wonderingly, I picked up the receiver.

"Hello."

"Miss Hunter?"

It was a woman's voice—hushed, excited.

"Yes, who is this?"

"Mrs. Wilsey!"

"Mrs. Wilsey?"

"Have you forgotten—that day in Jeggy Williams' car?"

Oh, I thought, The Snoop.

"No, Mrs. Wilsey," I said, without any feeling of pleasure, "I haven't forgotten you. What can I do for you?"

"I must see you at once. It's urgent. Can you meet me in town this evening?"

"Is it something you can't tell me now?"

"Yes. That is, I can't tell you over the phone. Someone might overhear us. And it's something important to you."

That someone was overhearing us right then, I did not doubt.

"Well, where shall we meet?"

"Tonight in front of the picture house. Say, after the first show?"

"All right, Mrs. Wilsey, I'll be there. But you know I won't have much time. The school bus doesn't wait beyond a certain hour."

"You won't need the bus. I'll have my car. This is Wilsey's night for bowling. I'll drive you home. Good-by."

"Very well."

I was sure I heard two sharp clicks after that, and I hung up reflectively. Why should anyone have been interested in that conversation? Then I shrugged. What was to be was to be.

The bus was crowded. Tuesday was a popular town night among the faculty.

Henrietta and George Mundin got into the bus at the last minute, and I noticed that her eyes were red-rimmed. Mundin leaned back against the leather cushions, ignoring his companion while allowing his eyes to rove over the occupants of the vehicle.

As we got out of the bus, the driver made his usual inquiries as to the exact time each of us would be ready to return.

"I'm bringing Miss Evangeline down to the town meeting," he announced, "but I don't have to call for her."

Cornelia Fiske flashed a glance at Mundin.

"I won't be coming back by bus, either," I said.

This innocent remark fell like a bombshell in their midst, but I managed to march toward the theater with what I supposed was dignity.

The lobby was a stuffy little place, but at least it offered me a comfortable seat. I waited there impatiently, watching the entrance. As time wore on, I began to experience a feeling of panic.

A sudden outpouring of people from the auditorium told me the movie had ended. The lobby was quite crowded now, and suddenly I felt a tug at my elbow.

"Here I am," said the high-pitched voice.

"I was beginning to think you had changed your mind about coming, Mrs. Wilsey."

"No danger of that, Miss Hunter. Come along—my car's outside."

She led me to a dilapidated contraption that rivaled Jeggy's.

"Where are we going?" I asked as the car heaved, grunted, and wheezed before finally bounding ahead.

"I'm taking you to my home. It's safer to talk there. Wilsey's out for the evening, and I figured a cup of tea in my kitchen is as good as you get anywhere."

The car drew up finally before a small frame house. It was a homey place inside, simply furnished and faultlessly clean.

"Mrs. Wilsey," I began, after she had taken me to the kitchen and started to prepare tea, "I can't stay long. We're not supposed to be out late. If I don't get back soon, the caretaker may lock me out."

"Just you bide your time," she said quietly, taking some cookies from a jar and arranging them on a plate. "Miss Perkins tells me there's a peck of trouble at the school this term—one lump or two?"

"No sugar, thank you."

"Slimming?"

After a few minutes of sipping her tea, she was ready for further conversation.

"I expect you know most everything that goes on, Miss Hunter, being up at the school all the time, but," here her voice grew hushed, "I wonder if there ain't some things you don't know."

"Please tell me why you sent for me?"

"Well, you know that Doctor Rudlow who runs the institution for loonies?"

"I thought he just ran a sanitarium."

"Same thing," she sniffed. "Well, anyhow, a few days ago I went up there. My Aunt Evvie's been there six months come Easter. I waited three whole weeks before the doctor gave me permission to see Evvie. When I got there the nurse stayed in the room with us the whole time. I admit I was kind of scarey—you never know, you know—I thought it was right nice of the doctor to be so considerate."

"Quite the usual procedure, I should think."

"Here's the point, Miss Hunter. I could swear on a stack of Bibles that my Aunt Evvie ain't batty at all."

I shifted uncomfortably. This was just the kind of story I might have imagined she had for me. But I was relieved.

"Sometimes, Mrs. Wilsey," I said pedantically, "it's hard for the layman to understand these cases. I am quite sure there would be no reason for Doctor Rudlow to keep your aunt unless she needed treatment."

"He's getting paid for it, ain't he?"

I looked at her, startled. The feeling of relief began to ebb slowly. Here was a thought not to be ignored. Why should a woman like that be in a private institution when her relatives were so obviously poor?

"Do you . . ."

"Pay for her? No, Miss Evangeline takes care of that."

"Miss Evangeline!"

"Yes. Evvie used to work at the school. Right nice of Miss Meredith, don't you think?"

"Of course," I said, rising, feeling I had now heard all that I needed to. "Well, what do you want of me?"

"I want you to see my aunt."

"You want me—good heavens! Mrs. Wilsey, you're requesting the impossible. I can't meddle in the affairs of others. If it were difficult for you to get the interview, what do you suppose Doctor Rudlow would say to a request of mine?"

"You could find a way," she insisted. "The nurse said sometimes some of the girls from the school go there to rest up."

"I suppose that's true," I admitted reluctantly.

"Couldn't you go just for—"

"Mrs. Wilsey," I said angrily, "you're asking me to risk my own position. That's too much. Please take me home now. The whole idea is preposterous. You brought me here under false pretenses, saying you had information which concerned me."

"I was just coming to that."

"Well, you will have to tell your story driving," I said, walking out of the house.

She followed close on my heels and we climbed into the car.

"Let's see, where was I?" she asked after she'd started the car.

"Your interview with your aunt had just ended."

"Oh, yes, well, while the nurse was locking the door, I peeked down the hall. A door opened, and who do you suppose came out of a room with the doctor?"

"I'm sure I can't guess."

"Helena Meredith."

I didn't show quite the surprise she had anticipated, but she went on.

"By the time the nurse was ready, the two of them had passed out of sight in the other direction. I got to wondering what Helena was doing there. It wasn't as though she'd been to the doctor's office. I knew that was on the first floor. Well, anyhow, the nurse took me down in the visitor's elevator. We got really chatty. Well, from one thing to another we got around to the school. I spoke of Miss Evangeline, and then said, careful-like, 'They say Miss Helena is doing poorly.' "

" 'I wouldn't know,' the nurse says, looking at me kind of hard and getting mighty unfriendly all of a sudden. 'And I wouldn't say,' she adds frightening-like. I was right glad when she left me at the front door. But, here's the main point—where you come in."

The machine swerved giddily as she turned to me.

"Watch out," I admonished.

"As soon as I was sure the nurse was out of sight, I stole back into the hall. 'I'm a law-abiding citizen,' I said to myself. 'No one is going to deprive me of my rights. And I have a right to know what goes on here.' The office door was open a mite, and I could hear the doctor talking. Guess I'd know his voice anywhere. Wouldn't you?"

I confessed that I would.

"At first I figured the doctor was talking to Helena, since I didn't see her leave the building. Then he said, "She's in splendid shape, Evangeline,' and of course I knew I was wrong. I peeked careful-like into the room. Doctor Rudlow was sitting behind his desk, talking on the telephone. He said, 'I guess your worries will soon be over. I know the signs.' I just felt he was talking about Helena, and you might say he was answering the question I put to the nurse. I can tell you I was relieved to learn Helena was all right. It wouldn't be so good for the school if one of the teachers went loco."

"That's nonsense," I said. "What would that have to do with the school?"

"You can't tell," she said, tipping her head to one side, and looking at me sagely. "Can't tell. Folks might get to remembering things about other—Merediths."

I was sure she was referring to Deborah Meredith, but had no intention of going into a discussion about this with her now. We were nearing the school gate now, and I wanted to hear the end of Mrs. Wilsey's tale.

"Did you leave after that?" I asked.

"Not quite. I was jest about to let the doctor know I was there when

I heard him say, 'How long must I wait? Well, what about the Horning girl? I tell you I'm anxious to make those tests now. It will revolutionize the whole field of psychiatry'—whatever that means. Then she must have said something and he answered, 'License or no license, what I need is the proper raw material to work with.'

"I didn't like the sound of his voice, Miss Hunter, and I don't know what he meant. But here's the part that will really get you. After a little more talk he asked, 'Any changes in Miss Hunter? She'd make a good subject.'"

Almost unconsciously, I seized my companion's arm.

"There, there, dearie," she said, giving me a kindly pat. "I 'spect that is a shock. I know. I couldn't stay after that. Somehow I just didn't feel like gabbing with that doctor, after all."

"Mrs. Wilsey," I said, trying to still a mounting terror, "please do me a favor. Discuss this matter with no one, not even your husband. What you learned for certain is that Miss Helena is well. The rest— why . . . you may have imagined something was wrong."

"That's what I try to tell myself, but then I remember there's bad blood in the Merediths. We don't trust the sisters, knowing the things about them we do."

"Please do as I suggested," I said and added a trifle too impulsively, since I had no plans yet, "perhaps next time you visit your aunt I will go along."

She brought the car to a halt outside the gate.

"Thank you, Miss Hunter," she said, wringing my hand. "I thought you would help. Good night, now, and God bless you."

"Aren't you driving me up to the house?" I asked, as she leaned over and opened the door beside me.

"Up to the main building!" she exclaimed. "Never! I don't hanker after any place where the dear departed are buried under the house."

"Good night, then," I said, "and thank you."

I laughed a trifle shakily as I pushed open the gate. What in the world had I thanked her for? And was she to be trusted? Perhaps she, also, was involved in Miss Evangeline's plan.

Chapter XIV

MRS. WILSEY's car drove off into the night as I went up the driveway. I wanted to down the little voice that kept insisting— those pills they gave you, the medicine the students hate, what of those so-called rest cures at the sanitarium?

And, above all, why was Evangeline, our miserly Headmistress, being so generous to a former employee? For Mrs. Wilsey's tale had rung true, and I did believe it.

The more I pondered the telephone conversation she had overheard, the more alarmed I grew.

At the top of the hill, I came upon Doctor Rudlow's car. It was empty, but its headlights burned brightly. Was the doctor bidding Evangeline a hurried good night, or had he been summoned on an emergency call?

I entered the building cautiously. The moment I was inside I knew something was wrong. The air rustled with disturbed whisperings. From above came the sound of muffled footsteps. Doors closed hastily on hushed voices. Hardly was my hand on the balustrade when two tall figures were silhouetted in the archway and then stepped out onto the landing. They were heading in my direction.

Eager to avoid a meeting with Evangeline and Rudlow, I stealthily stole down toward the back door. The passageway was in darkness, but I felt my way along the wall. Instinct guided me to the rear of the building. The door to the back stairs was closed. It was not only closed, but it was locked.

The front of the house was silent when I returned, but a dim light still burned in the entryway. I slowly mounted the staircase nearest me. When I was a few steps from the landing, I heard a man speaking. Two figures moved partially into view, and halted midway between the gallery and the stairs.

"Wait, did you hear a sound just then?"

It was Evangeline who asked the question. I stood there hardly daring to breathe.

"Nonsense," Rudlow said in answer to Evangeline's question. "You're a little jittery after what just occurred. As I was saying, she didn't have the reaction I was expecting."

"You cannot blunder in this manner, Emile. You will ruin my school."

The doctor laughed. "It is not I who have blundered along that line, my dear."

"What do you mean?"

"Let it pass. There are more important matters to discuss. Must you always consider the school and the Merediths first?"

"That is all that counts. Everyone is not interested in becoming a guinea pig, even for the sake of psychoanalysis."

"I will not bring disgrace on your rogues' gallery. I'll wager the old man would have given me *carte blanche*. There was a wicked gleam in his eye!"

"Why you—" Evangeline's voice was metallic, "you're not fit to discuss my father, let alone criticize him."

"I had nothing against Silas Meredith except the fact that the woman I would choose to marry happens to be in love with him!"

"How dare you!"

"Do you think I draw the line in my analyses? I know all about your visits to his tomb, the hours you spend there alone, the way your expression changes when you look at his picture."

"You don't know what you're talking about—you fraud—I'll have you thrown out of Seacliffe, out of the country—"

"Softly, softly, Evangeline. I have no wish to do you harm. You can't condemn a man for being jealous. Perhaps I have been thinking of your interests, too. I sometimes wonder who will be the next heir to this estate?"

"The descent has always been in the direct line, and so it must continue to be."

"Your father should have had a son."

"But he didn't. Therefore, the descent must come through me, the eldest daughter."

"You and I would make a remarkable couple. Have you no feeling for me, Evangeline?"

"You speak like a fool. I'm tired, Emile. Please go."

"How can a woman like you, capable of such great passions, have escaped the—shall I say, stigma of love?"

"Love is only an emotion, a display of weakness. However, this much I will say, Emile. Had my father left the entire estate to me, as he had often promised. I would be free to select a husband of my own choice. As things are, there cannot be two mistresses at Meredith Hall."

They slowly descended the staircase on the opposite side of the hall.

In the corridor above, I met Diana Marden coming from the lavatory. The pallor of her face startled me, and I recalled my earlier premonition that something was wrong in the dormitories.

"Diana," I whispered, "why was Doctor Rudlow called?"

"Because of Eliza Horning," she said starkly, dropping her supercilious manner toward me for the first time.

The front door slammed below. In a few minutes Evangeline would be upon us.

"I'll tell you in the morning."

For a long time that night I lay awake haunted by what I had overheard. I could not tie it all together, and yet, somehow, I knew it was a part of the same picture.

Next morning I found Eliza still in her bed. Even under the blankets I could sense the rigidness of her body and her eyes were stricken with the fear which I had seen so often in Elaine's.

"Isn't it time you were getting up for breakfast, Eliza?" I began pleasantly.

"No," she said tensely, "I can't. I won't get up. I won't leave this bed. No one can make me."

I sat down on the bed, and her body shrank from me.

"Go away, Miss Hunter, please go away."

"Tell me, Eliza, what's wrong?"

"Everything, everything."

Gently I managed to extract the story. She spoke haltingly and wept copiously.

"I—I get so—so many colds, you know. Doctor Rudlow said it was psychic with me. He asked if I would like to be psychoanalyzed."

At this point Diana joined us, and her friend did not object to her being there but went on with her narrative.

"At first I thought it would be fun to be psychoanalyzed. Di and I always like fortune tellers, and—"

"Tell the truth," cut in Diana. "You got a crush on Svengali Rudlow like a lot of the other girls, and he used you for all you were worth."

Eliza made no attempt to defend herself, but became so hysterical that Diana continued where she left off.

"Rudlow experimented on Eliza. He didn't interest himself in me because he discovered I wasn't receptive. And about a week ago Eliza began to get all mixed up about herself. She begged him to stop, but he wouldn't."

"Now I'm all mixed up," Eliza cried, "just as if I were two people. He says that's part of the treatment. He says because my mind was sick, my body was sick, and now I'm afraid, Miss Hunter, I'm afraid! I'm afraid I'm losing my mind! Doctor Rudlow thinks I should go to the sanitarium or else visit him each day for treatments. But I don't want to go. He's the one who made me sick. I know! I know!"

"Nonsense, Eliza. You're perfectly well and normal. You're tired and frightened, that's all."

"Help me, Miss Hunter," Eliza pleaded, "help me! I can't bear it any more!"

She burst into wild sobs.

Mademoiselle came into the dormitory while I was still there. I had had little to do with this small, sad-faced woman who, burdened with care and responsibility, displayed none of the traditional French *joie de vivre*.

"*Pauvre enfant,*" said Mademoiselle, looking toward Eliza.

"If she could only get away from here for a little while."

"Precisely. I have made the arrangements. There is a conference of the *Alliance Française* in Middlebury which I am to attend. I thought I would take her with me since she is an outstanding French scholar. I have given Miss Evangeline the assurance that it will be beneficial to the school's reputation."

Her lips trembled, and something like a smile flickered across them and swiftly vanished.

All during breakfast I thought of one thing—Eleanor Vaughn's death and the pills Rudlow had prescribed for me. If I could prove that the medicine he had ordered for a cold was a powerful drug, I would have proof to support the suspicions I had been harboring. But how could I go to the village drugstore to find out the ingredients? The chemist might be in Rudlow's employ. Who was there to be trusted?

A sudden thought struck me—Homer Fiske. Homer Fiske had always been kind to me at the faculty meetings, and he had a degree in chemistry.

On my way out of the dining room, I noticed that Homer was not at the faculty table. He had probably gone to the city. Cornelia Fiske confirmed my suspicions. Homer had gone out of town, and would not be back until evening.

Perhaps, I could go to Philip.

Hardly had the gong sounded for first class when I found myself hurrying down the corridor.

As I came to the last room, I heard Philip's voice coming through the open doorway. I paused at the threshold. When he turned his head and saw me, he excused himself from his class and shut the door after him.

"Miss Hunter," he said formally, "I thought I had made myself quite clear to you. There is nothing more for us to say to each other."

"But Philip, I must talk to you! You must listen to me this once. There's something you should know."

I saw him stiffen, and glancing sideways, caught sight of a sallow-faced housemaid. Everyone knew that she was one of Evangeline's spies.

We waited until she was out of sight, and then Philip looked down at me again.

"My schedule is full today," he said in an impersonal tone. "And in the future, please do not disturb me when I have a class." He disappeared into the room, closed the door.

The March morning dragged on endlessly. I would have appreciated a few hours all to myself and my misery, but unfortunately I had promised Helena Meredith to work with her on her portrait that afternoon.

The portrait was almost completed. I had followed the general outline of the original sketch. I had kept the sea as a background. The weather had prevented me from working on this outdoors, but I knew I could put the sea in later.

Helena appeared unduly elated that afternoon as she stood rigidly on the small platform.

"At last I, too, will have a portrait in the gallery, just like the others," she said. "No one can prevent this one from hanging there."

"Is there any reason why your portrait shouldn't be in the gallery?"

"I've had my portrait painted many times, but Evangeline refused to have any of the others hung. She found fault with each one. But this time . . ." She squinted at the painting, and then added unexpectedly, "I wonder how Philip will like it."

"Why especially Philip?"

She wheeled on me rapturously.

"Someday Philip and I are going to be married."

The paint brush slipped from my fingers and fell to the floor.

"We planned this long ago. When we were children, and Philip used to—used to protect me from Evangeline, I always said I would marry him when we grew up."

"And is he going to protect you from Evangeline now?"

"Yes, he will protect me now. He must. Father always believed the awful things Evangeline said about me. I never had a chance. She forced her attentions on him, but he never really liked her any better than he did me. She never has quite forgiven his leaving an equal part of the estate to me. She always told him I wasn't well enough to handle my own affairs, but he didn't listen to her. And as Philip's wife, I will be the real mistress of Meredith Hall. Two-thirds of the estate will be mine, and half the income from the school. When that day comes— when that day comes—"

"Yes?"

"Evangeline will see that she can't rule me any longer. Perhaps the time will come when she will have to go."

Chapter XV

L ATE THE next evening, Eliza Horning returned without Mademoiselle, and there was a rumor the French teacher had secured a new position. Mademoiselle had not returned for her clothes, and she had requested that they be sent to a new address. It was announced at breakfast to faculty and students alike that, for the time being, no substitute would be found for Mademoiselle and Miss Evangeline herself would take over the French classes. Despite persistent proddings by the students, Eliza refused to give any information and went about her activities in a morose and serious manner.

I lay on my bed that afternoon, thinking about Eliza. Then I thought of Doctor Rudlow and his pills. I had neglected to go to Homer Fiske. Now was the time to have the small, white globes analyzed. If only something could be proved against Rudlow . . .

Learning from Mary, who stopped in for a moment, that Mr. Fiske had just returned from the city in time for dinner, I planned to see him at the table.

As I entered the dining room, I saw Homer at the opposite end of the long hall, but was unable to talk to him during the course of the entire meal. He ate very little and seemed, from where I was seated, to be intensely angry. He was engaged in conversation with Evangeline at their table and every so often he would glance at Cornelia. Now and then I could see him move his head violently, and frequently he shook a finger at his wife. All at once he got up and stalked furiously from the room. Cornelia nodded her head pensively after his departing figure. Then she turned toward Evangeline. Even from my rather remote position I could see an exchange of glances between the two women.

After dinner, we all went in to see the Latin play. And as soon as that was finished, I slipped unobtrusively out the side door which also served as an extra entrance to a hallway leading to the kitchen. I wanted to find Homer Fiske. The most likely place to find him would be in his laboratory.

I passed a high hedge and had almost crossed its length when the sound of voices stopped me. Although the people were hidden from view, from their voices I knew one of them to be Diana Marden. I heard her say something in which "love" was repeated many times. Then I heard a young male voice say, "Of course, I love you. I'll always love you."

So this was the answer to the mystery which had cost me two weeks' salary. Well, there was enough trouble at Meredith Hall without my telling on Diana now. If she were in love, even if it were only puppy love, I wasn't going to disturb her. Suddenly a twig snapped beneath my feet. I heard a frightened gasp from the other side of the hedge, and then I ran swiftly down the path into the shadows.

I rounded a turn in the path and found two people standing in the night gloom. They had not heard me approaching, for they were busily engaged in some sort of argument. The woman was pleading.

"I didn't spy on you, George, honestly I didn't. But I was jealous. You know that I love you."

"Then give me those letters, Henrietta."

"I haven't any letters," she sobbed. "Please believe me. I looked for them, but it was no use . . . Someone took them!"

She sniffed and started to sob again.

"George, you have been drinking again—"

Mundin swore under his breath. "Well, what of it? I have a right, haven't I? Drinking oneself to death is a much better way to go than the way Eleanor did—" There was a pause, then—"I was a fool to have written any notes to her in the first place. I'll admit that, but it wasn't Eleanor's fault. She would never have used them against me.

It must have been Evangeline who found them. That fiend! Yes, she must have the letters. She's capable of anything!"

Henrietta's voice rose a little.

"And Eleanor Vaughn was out to get all she could, too!"

"Nonsense, you were jealous. You even say so yourself. Besides— while we're about it—I don't want you to be hanging around me all the time and telling me what to do. I'll drink whenever I please."

Afraid that I might be detected if I lingered any longer, I crawled through the hedge and took a short cut to the stone house.. There was a light in the window. I entered the laboratory to find Homer busily engaged at a table, test tube in hand.

"May I come in?"

"Why, yes, Miss Hunter, certainly come in. I was wondering when you were going to pay me a visit."

I looked around the room.

"You have a fine place here. It's one of the best school laboratories I've ever seen."

"Indeed it is, but it wouldn't be if Evangeline had her way. I spent a good part of my own money getting the apparatus and the essential things to work with. Everyone here makes money his God. They worship the wrong things, Miss Hunter, money and tradition. They can't see that science is supreme." His hand touched my shoulder in fatherly counsel. "This place will change you, too, my dear. Better get away. Yes, better get away as soon as possible."

Here was another warning—a friendly one, yes, but all the more pronounced.

My hand stole into my pocket and touched the packet of pills. I took out the little package.

"What have you there, Miss Hunter? Pills? Of medicinal substance, no doubt."

"Yes . . . They were given me by Dr. Rudlow. I would like to have them analyzed. I've reason to believe that they're not really what they're supposed to be."

Homer eyed me for a moment, and then spoke slowly, "Why, yes, if you wish, Miss Hunter. But it will take some time. However, I'll see what I can do."

Then the old man seemed to hesitate.

"Why do you suspect this? Didn't you say that Doctor Rudlow gave them to you?"

"Yes, he did. But I have reasons to believe as I do. Nevertheless, if you don't want to do this . . ."

I was a little afraid that I had been wrong in my judgment of Homer Fiske. I held my breath and waited. He went to a sink and washed his hands in a preoccupied manner.

"If you want the medicine to be examined, I'll do it for you, Miss

Hunter. Personally—" his voice was a whisper, "I don't think too much of Doctor Rudlow, myself."

This was certainly my opening.

"He is rather peculiar, isn't he? That's one of the reasons I want the pills tested. And I'm inclined to agree with you regarding his professional status. Do you know where Doctor Rudlow practiced before he came here?"

"In Philadelphia, I believe. He came here a year or two before old Silas died. According to Evangeline, Rudlow is going to be a great psychiatrist someday. She insists this will add to the prestige of the school."

He gave a little laugh and brushed his chin. But then a gray pallor came over his countenance, and I saw him grow dizzy. I tried to steady him and succeeded in getting him to a chair. I rushed to the sink and got a glass of water which I gave to him. He sipped it slowly, and after a few moments, he lifted his head, and his eyes peered weakly over the horn-rimmed spectacles.

"I'm all right now," he managed. "Just one of those spells. They come every once in a while."

"Have you seen a doctor, Mr. Fiske?"

He did not answer but instead stood up.

"I think a little air would do me good."

"We went out into the night. Our progress was slow, and we were rather long in returning to the Hall. As we came within the shadow of the building, we found Rudlow's car standing in its usual place near the front entrance.

"He's here all the time lately, causing disturbances in the dormitory again, I suppose."

"Yes," my companion's voice came back weakly, "there must be something going on. Just the way there was before she died."

"Who?"

"Eleanor Vaughn."

Homer stopped abruptly. We were in the dimly lighted hall now, and Cornelia Fiske loomed out of the shadows to greet us.

"I was wondering when you were going to return, Homer," Cornelia said in a voice that bordered on sarcasm. "Why do you insist on working at night on those useless experiments, especially when you are so tired?" She turned to me. "Of course, he was in the workshop, wasn't he, Miss Hunter?"

I said that he had been but said nothing of Homer's attack. But she must have surmised something there in the vestibule, for she said, "The doctor is here. Perhaps it would be a wise thing to see him before he goes."

Homer snorted, "What doctor?"

There were faint footsteps, and all of us instinctively looked up. The doctor and Evangeline were beginning to descend the staircase and as yet had not perceived us below them.

Cornelia did not answer her husband but hurriedly turned to me. "Let's go to the kitchen, Miss Hunter, and have a cup of tea. I'm sure we could all use a warm drink."

"I'm going to bed," Homer said.

We moved down the hallway, passing the front part of the house without making our presence known to the two descending the stairway. I thought it rather odd that Homer should follow us after saying that he was going to retire, but understood the reason when I remembered the back stair to the next story. He too, did not care to meet Evangeline and her companion. Another puzzling thought came to my mind. Why had Mrs. Fiske been so anxious not to be seen in the vestibule? Why the sudden offer of tea?

As we made our way down the long ill-lighted corridor, we passed several of the smaller sitting rooms. A lamp was burning in one of these, and we could see Helena sitting stiffly in a rocking chair. Her movement was a slow rhythm, her eyes stared straight ahead. I thought it best to go by without speaking, although Mrs. Fiske called out a greeting to her. But there was no answer, and we went on to the kitchen.

Homer left us at the rear stairwell.

"Good night, Miss Hunter," he said in a tired voice. "We shall have to get together soon for another chat."

Homer trudged upstairs.

Cornelia looked at me, shaking her head in her husband's direction. "Sometimes it seems that he won't be here with us much longer."

We went into the kitchen.

"I haven't been down here like this making tea," Cornelia said, "since —since that time with Eleanor. One never knows which are the last moments of one's life. Perhaps it is better that way, though. But no— Eleanor certainly didn't seem despondent. She never gave away the fact that she was contemplating suicide. If she knew that she was going to die, I wasn't aware of it."

Cornelia shrugged her shoulders as if she were through with the subject of Eleanor Vaughn, but I decided to press her further.

"Mrs. Fiske, the last time we two were alone, you said there was something extraordinary about Eleanor's good fortune in obtaining a position here. Just what did you mean?"

"Well, she was talented enough, I guess. But she was a crafty one. I don't see why Evangeline stood for her. I wouldn't have trusted her too far—that vixen!"

Just then I caught sight of the heavy oaken door, the one that led into the awful compartment used now as a pantry closet. With difficulty, I managed to turn away, but not before Mrs. Fiske had seen the troubled look on my face.

"It's a strange thing about that closet. Eleanor Vaughn would never go near it, although she was brazen enough about other things!"

Mrs. Fiske now went to a cupboard and took out cups and saucers. Her back was to me as she spoke again.

"I think you will find some cake in the pantry closet. Will you go and see? I'll take some tea up to Homer."

I shot a glance at the sinister aperture. My feet were lead, and I did not move. Mrs. Fiske turned around.

"She said—Oh, Miss Hunter, if you are afraid—"

I felt a coward. "I'll get it," I said.

I went to the yawning doorway, moved into the empty blackness until I found a light. Feverishly I searched for the cake and after a moment or two, found some. I turned. The closet door was moving slowly, almost imperceptibly; it was closing in on me.

I grabbed the cake and rushed toward the narrowing exit. I screamed. I flung myself against the heavy closing door. Crying and going almost blind with fear, I beat savagely upon the thick wooden panels.

Then something must have happened. A minute passed as I steadied myself and stepped back into the kitchen. I thought that I could hear the sound of someone running through the dark dining room. Then slowly the room spun around and the darkness deepened and soon there was no light at all.

Sometime later I awakened in my room. The doctor was bending over me, and he was talking to some indistinguishable gray form behind him.

"A case of nerves," I heard him say. "She will feel better when these pills take effect."

Take effect! I tried desperately to rise and to cry out that I did not want those hideous pills. But my body was weak and my mind was dulled and the voices became lower and indistinct. I felt myself sinking, sinking. My eyelids were lids of iron. I gave up the struggle.

Chapter XVI

WHOSE FOOTSTEPS had I heard running through the darkened dining room? Cornelia's? Evangeline's? Helena's? This was the first question I asked myself when I awoke. But I did not know the answer.

I waited for Homer's report with increasing apprehension. Now that there was a possibility—a faint one to be sure—that Rudlow might prove to be Evangeline's Achilles' heel, I could not rest in peace until I knew.

Homer's unexpected summons to a neighboring city for a period of three days almost drove me to distraction, and I spent the interval in planning what I would do in the event that Rudlow proved to be guilty. The police would know what to do about the doctor, I reasoned, were I to prove that he had prescribed medicine injurious to my health.

One day, my third and last morning class had assembled and were already seated, pencils poised over copybooks, when I had concluded a brief survey of my lecture notes. "Today," I advised them, "we will begin study of the greatest of all Florentine painters—Leonardo da Vinci."

Instantly all eyes flew to the very fine Matisse which hung on the wall between the windows. There were a few ejaculations of surprise, and I caught a look of bewilderment on several faces, as the girls whispered among themselves.

"It's gone," cried Edith Fenton.

"What became of the Mona Lisa?" chimed in Margaret Henning.

"Someone removed it," said Veronica Jennings. "I noticed that months ago."

"So did we," chorused a group of students.

"What is this all about?" I demanded, turning to Diana Marden, who seemed fairly well informed on all occurrences at the school.

"There was a painting of the Mona Lisa here," she explained. "It belonged to Eleanor Vaughn. She removed it herself just before—before Christmas, and hung the Matisse in its place."

At that moment I could find nothing strange in the fact that one painting had been substituted for another, and that the Mona Lisa did not appear to be in the studio any longer.

When the hour drew to a close, I could hardly contain my impatience to be off to the laboratory. Homer had told me on his return the day before that he would be ready for me this morning. To my surprise Diana Marden did not leave with the other students, but hovered uncertainly about my desk.

"May I have a moment, Miss Hunter?"

"Can what you have to say wait? I'm pressed for time. Mr. Fiske is waiting for me."

"Then let me walk along with you part of the way. What I have to say won't take long."

I couldn't refuse, and we left the studio together.

"I—I want to thank you," she faltered, "for being so square about Bob and me. I know we were breaking rules, and that you saw us together the other night, but we love each other so much."

"I didn't think of it again," I said. "I've forgotten all about it."

"You're a dear," she exclaimed, squeezing my arm. And then,

penitently, "I wish I hadn't treated you in such a beastly way—reporting your meetings with Mr. James to Miss Evangeline, I mean. I was angry about your having taken Eleanor's place."

"Why Diana!" I could hardly believe my ears. "I'm glad you've come to me. I really have minded your antagonism. After all, I couldn't change the situation."

"I know. I see that now, or rather," she confessed ruefully, "Bob made me see it that way."

As we walked up the path the girl seemed to be turning something over and over in her mind.

"Miss Hunter," she said finally. "Did you know that Eleanor Vaughn was an illegitimate child?"

"No. Nobody told me that."

"I thought knowing that might help you," Diana said.

Help me? How? I could not understand what Diana was implying.

"I'm not interested in Eleanor Vaughn's past," I said guardedly, "and assuredly, I'm not anxious to besmirch her memory with foul gossip."

Diana looked offended.

"It's not gossip. I'd never spread false tales about her. Eleanor told me that herself . . . I don't blame you for not wanting to take me into your confidence, but if you ever decide to change your mind, I may be able to help you."

Homer Fiske was alone in the laboratory when I entered. He was measuring some liquid into a test tube with great concentration.

It seemed hours before he completed this experiment, which I had the feeling he could ordinarily have carried out in short order. Today he was acting like a man in a trance, uncertain of his movements, even clumsy. I tiptoed across to the table, and perched on one of the round stools lined up around it. How thin Homer had grown since I had first met him! His collar stood away from a scrawny, gnarled throat, and his grayish cheeks were cavernous.

Suddenly, the tube slipped from his shaking fingers, and dashed into smithereens on the hard floor.

"I can't understand it. I can't understand what happened. I must have made a mistake," the poor man mumbled, half to himself as he stooped to pick up the pieces of glass.

"Let me do that, Mr. Fiske."

"Oh, Miss Hunter—good morning. I suppose you saw what just happened."

"Yes. Accidents can happen to anyone."

"But you can't afford accidents in this kind of work. We might have been killed."

He continued to mumble in this vein to himself while I cleaned the floor. A few minutes later, however, the entire incident seemed to have slipped his memory, and I found him bent over a large black notebook, scribbling furiously.

Just as I was about to recall his attention to my presence, he spoke to me.

"I report all the failures and the successes here. Lately, they are all failures."

"Well, they won't always be . . . Mr. Fiske," I said, seeing that he was about to repeat his experiment, "I'm sorry to take up your time, but haven't you that report for me now?"

"Report?"

"Yes, you know—on those pills I asked you to analyze."

"Oh, oh yes. I'll get around to that as soon as I have a chance."

"Why, Mr. Fiske, you know it's urgent that I have the report—because of Doctor Rudlow. You promised to help me."

"Did I? I—I should not have— There can be nothing wrong with those pills."

"How do you know? Have you analyzed them already?"

"No, no, I haven't analyzed them. Too busy. Classes all morning— It's just that I am convinced a man like Doctor Rudlow knows what he's doing."

"I thought I could count on you. Now I see you're just like all the rest."

He chewed his lips nervously. "I will make that test for you. Of course, I will. Never said I wouldn't. But I know you are wasting your time as well as mine. Don't be impatient. I'll send for you as soon as the analysis has been made."

Suddenly his whole body quivered. He steadied himself against the table as beads of sweat stood out on his forehead.

"Mr. Fiske," I said contritely, fearful that this interview had been too much for him, "are you ill?"

"I'll be all right."

I shall never forget the serious expression on his tired face as he came over and took me gently by the arm.

"Please," he said, " do as I told you the other night. Find yourself a nice position—someplace else—someplace far away from here."

"Yes," I said patiently, "I will do that. Only first you must help me. There are certain problems I must clear up before I leave."

"I'll help you," he said, but he looked about vacantly and his thoughts seemed to be wandering again. "I'll help you."

Far from reassured, and troubled about the state of his health, I left the laboratory.

All through lunch I was preoccupied with the problem of what to do now that help from Homer Fiske seemed so uncertain. Perhaps I ought to send the pills to Doctor Byles, our old family physician.

Lunch over, I hurried to my dresser. I searched beneath the pile of slips until my fingers found the little bottle. Then I gave a gasp of dismay—the bottle was empty!

Someone was keeping pace with my movements. This discovery brought a fresh realization of my increasingly precarious position at Meredith Hall. Whoever had preceded me here had been very efficient, even to the removal of the druggist's name from the bottle. I knew a moment of panic wherein I wanted to rush to the closet, pack my things and escape. I remember carrying on a strange soliloquy. They're after me. I must run away. Elaine had warned me. They had all warned me.

I flew to the door and locked it, fearing that someone might come into my room now and catch me unawares. Nervously I stared at the closet. Had the door been open when I entered, or was it opening now? Was I going mad? No, the only madness was to stay! But I still had one chance left—the pills I had left with Homer. Homer would gladly return them to me—if he still had them in his possession.

Erasing further doubt from my mind, I ran back to the laboratory. At the door of the roundhouse I was halted by the sound of angry voices. Suspecting that this quarrel might be of concern to me, I stole around to an open window through which the furious accents were issuing and, pressing my body close to the stone frame, peered cautiously inside.

Evangeline Meredith was there with Cornelia Fiske. Evangeline stood with her back to the test tube rack where I had found Homer a few hours before. Her eyes burned with anger, but a cruel smile played about her lips.

Cornelia looked as though she had returned from town in a rush. She was loaded down with packages, and her hat hung askew on her head.

"What happened to Homer?" she was crying.

Evangeline stared at her frigidly and she flapped Homer's small, black notebook back and forth in her hands.

"He's had a stroke," she said.

"A stroke! Oh, God."

The anguish in Cornelia's voice was genuine.

"Yes. One side of his body is completely paralyzed."

"He was all right when I left. Something must have happened to bring on the attack."

"Yes. He received a shock."

Cornelia looked at her cousin with eyes of hatred and suspicion.

"You did something to him! You killed him."

"Hush, Cornelia. Someone might hear you. Homer is still alive. If you were so concerned over his welfare, why didn't you go straight to his room to see for yourself? Mrs. Hawkins must have mentioned that Homer was ill when you came in."

"She didn't say it was so serious and I saw you walking in this direction. I wanted to find out what you were after—in here!"

"It is quite customary for me to make a weekly tour of inspection."

"To go prying into his experiments, you mean!"

"Really, Cornelia, sometimes you speak like a fishwife. Surely, you don't believe Homer has any ideas for me to steal."

She laughed and suddenly tossed the notebook to her cousin. The book fell at Mrs. Fiske's feet, but she didn't stoop to pick it up.

"Just read this record of a wasted life. Still I don't blame you for being concerned over Homer's welfare. Part of your income depends on his being alive."

"You can't deprive him of his position. Uncle Silas saw to that."

"I don't think you realize how ill Homer is."

"A stroke is not serious."

"Unfortunately a second stroke generally proves fatal. Why didn't you tell us about the first? Never mind," Evangeline wheeled and held up a warning hand, "I know the answer. You recalled the special clause in father's will."

"What are you driving at?"

" 'As long as the instructors remain at the Hall,' " Evangeline intoned, " 'never leaving it for more than two weeks at a time, they are entitled to the benefits of my estate.' I am afraid, my dear cousin, in your desire to live up to the letter of the law you neglected to give your husband the proper treatment. It is you who have destroyed him."

"Silas stole my father's birthright."

"A modern Esau. To the victor belongs the spoils, according to modern philosophy, my dear cousin. Let us not delve into the past. Your father had the same opportunity as mine, but he lacked my father's wits."

"You mean he lacked old Silas' evil genius."

"You will live to regret those words," Evangeline said. "They are ill-spoken by one who had every reason to be grateful to Silas Meredith. Father was interested in Homer—Heaven alone knows why!—I never expected him to amount to anything and therefore cannot share your disappointment."

Mrs. Fiske's hands clutched the packages until the knuckles were white, but she said nothing.

Evangeline went on, "It didn't take you long to find out that your poor, ineffectual Homer would never set the world aflame, save through an error. It was then you thought of my father, and prevailed upon him with lies and tears to give you both positions here at the school. You have been collecting doubly from the estate all these years."

"You would look at it that way. You can't help judging others by yourself."

"A very pretty act, Cornelia. But I know all about your attempt to take out insurance on your husband's life without his knowledge, even to the forging of his signature in a letter naming you as beneficiary.

Had those plans gone through, I don't think you would have regretted learning he was ill."

"Who are your spies?" Cornelia asked. "How do you know all these things? Sometimes I think you're not human."

"On the contrary, cousin, it is you who surprise me. My congratulations on all your clever designs. That was quick thinking on your part to arrange for both salary checks to be made payable to you. Homer was astounded at the actual sum of money you have been receiving."

"Homer! What does he know about this?"

"I had to tell him the truth. He began making some unpleasant accusations about me, and when he resorted to threats I felt it necessary to expose you out of self-defense."

The packages slipped from Cornelia's hands.

"You told him . . . knowing that he was ill."

"Again, my dear Cornelia, you are to blame. You should have warned us of his condition."

"Homer will live. He must," Mrs. Fiske cried. "I'll explain everything to him." She stooped hastily to retrieve her packages. "You think you hold the whip hand, but it's your father who holds all of us in check, to this day. Even you are held back by the restrictions of his will. You would like to get rid of all of us. But you can't."

"You're quite right," said Evangeline. "I would like to be rid of all of you. If there had been any means within my power I would have done so long ago. Fortunately," she turned slowly toward the window, and I dipped swiftly out of sight, "if you give people enough rope," she said, "yes, enough rope—"

"What do you mean?"

"If Homer lives he will insist you leave the school. He refuses to remain here any longer."

"I won't go. I have a right to remain here!"

"Calm yourself, Cornelia. There is little likelihood of Homer's survival. You have nothing to fear on that score. Of course, if he should survive, you could not risk going against his will. Remember forgery is a criminal offense."

Mrs. Fiske did not answer that, but rushed out through the door and up toward the main house. A few minutes later Evangeline followed, sweeping regally across the lawn.

I waited, clinging close to the side of the house long after she was out of sight. Then I searched the laboratory.

I should have known that the pills would not be in the laboratory any longer.

Homer Fiske died that night. I had been prepared for the event, but his death came as a shock to the students.

Evangeline's grief at the funeral was a revolting display of hypocrisy, but harder to endure were Cornelia's tears.

* * *

Chapter XVII

* * *

A STRANGE quietude settled over the Hall after Homer Fiske's death. But beneath the surface of normal school life and mourning, continual undercurrents of hatred seethed. And they all seemed to culminate in an increasing display of hostility toward me.

My relations with Diana had improved, of course. Yet even this was a hollow victory. Since her cordial overtures toward me were immediately seconded by the majority of students who followed her leadership, Diana now regarded herself as my benefactor. She brazenly expected me to reward her metamorphosis by becoming a fellow-conspirator in her rule-breaking. I grew to dread patrol duty, for I could no longer go on closing my eyes to Diana's nocturnal escapades.

Meanwhile, Helena Meredith hounded me constantly for her portrait. I found consolation in the thought that the completing of the painting would mean the end of long sessions in her company. For, even when I was putting in the background and no longer needed her to sit for me, she insisted on watching me.

The day I finished painting the background, Evangeline joined us. We were outdoors close to the edge of the precipice, because I wanted an unobstructed view of the sea. It was all there on the canvas now—the gray torrents of water lashing the rocky coast and the slight figure of Helena, a fury in this savage setting.

"Helena resembles her mother," Evangeline remarked after a long silence. "I take after the Meredith branch of the family."

There was no mistaking the disparagement of her sister, and I wondered what else Evangeline saw in the painting.

"She has her father's eyes," I said.

"Not at all. There isn't a suggestion of our side of the Meredith family in Helena's face normally. If there is in the painting, your work is inaccurate."

"Oh, but there isn't," Helena said. "You will permit the portrait to hang in the gallery, Evangeline, won't you?"

"Of course, why not? Miss Hunter has done remarkably well. The likeness is unmistakable."

"It's all finished now, isn't it?" Helena asked.

"There are still a few touches, but that won't take long."

"It mustn't take long. Finish it this week. The picture needs to be framed and I want it hung before Easter. There will be many visitors at the Passion performance we always give, and they inevitably go through the gallery."

I decided to devote the following afternoon to the final touches.

Just after my three o'clock class had been dismissed, I went to the closet. The canvas was in its customary place protected by a cloth covering. As the cloth fell away from the portrait, I cried out, horrified. Someone had slashed it in a dozen places.

But this was insane! Who had done it? What was to be done? Helena would go raging mad. I must hide the picture until I could copy it.

I hurried to the front door and turned the key. Just as I was carrying the portrait to the east room closet, there was a knocking on the door. I waited, tense. Someone called my name. A woman's voice.

The knocking became more insistent.

"Yes," I called and, flinging wide the door, confronted a most unexpected visitor—Henrietta Valentine!

After a brief pause, Henrietta said, "I came here primarily, Miss Hunter, to offer you an apology."

"What for?"

"It's a little awkward to explain," she simpered, her eyes opening wide in a helpless, baby-like stare, "but—do you remember the night you arrived?"

Could I ever forget it, I thought, and, then suddenly, while looking at Henrietta, realization dawned on me.

"This may sound strange to you, but I came back from the city to search the studio for—for some letters. I didn't expect to meet anyone. When I heard the door open I was sure it was Evangeline, and I was afraid. I've always been afraid of her."

"When did you find out it wasn't Evangeline?"

"We-ell, that's the strange part of it. I didn't know the girl in the sea-house was you until the faculty tea. That night I waited outside the studio. You see, I hadn't found what I came for, and I wanted to go back again after you left. I looked in the window. Then—well, I thought I was seeing a ghost, and—and I didn't stay." She began fumbling in her handbag. "I have a sketch here of Eleanor Vaughn. A self-sketch. When you look at it, you will see why everyone mistook you for her at first."

I took the sketch from her. Now I would see her, myself—what she had been.

"How she loved making self-portraits and handing them out to the men," Henrietta went on. "Always in color, of course. She was very vain about her red hair."

And at last I was looking at Eleanor Vaughn. Her face held me, not merely because of its beauty, but because I did resemble her, and because I felt that I had met Eleanor Vaughn before.

"May I keep this?" I asked. "I would like to look at it again! You understand. I've heard so much about her, and—"

An idea came to me as my eyes met Henrietta's. The look of frustration I read there craved sympathy and understanding. Here was someone who might know what went on behind the scenes. She appeared friendly, perhaps I could make her talk.

"Henrietta," I began, drawing a chair over to the fireplace, and seating myself opposite her, "why should Eleanor Vaughn have committed suicide?"

The question disconcerted the woman.

"I'm sure that I don't—that nobody really knows, except Evangeline. I don't think she was really sorry it happened. I don't thing she wants to see Philip James ever get married. She watches him like a hawk. As a matter of fact, I don't believe she wants any of the heirs to marry."

"Why? Has she done anything to make you feel that way?"

"It's not what she does, it's what she says. The power of suggestion goes a long way. Evangeline is never obvious. She knows how I feel about George, and yet she insists on telling me repeatedly that he'll never marry me."

Henrietta's blue eyes filled with tears.

"What makes her so sure?"

"The way he treats me, for one thing. Then, of course, she knows about that time—"

"What time?"

"—When George and I were in college. We've known each other since we were children. I never wanted to—to—but he promised he would marry me afterward. I thought he would keep his word, and then I found out it was just another one of his lies."

"How does Evangeline know such intimate details about you?"

"She knows about all of our private lives. That's how she keeps us in her power."

"Real blackmail."

Henrietta nodded.

"Evangeline knows she could prevent me from getting a position anywhere else. Oh, I don't mind so much about that. It's only George who matters to me."

This time Henrietta began to sob.

"Tell me about Eleanor Vaughn," I persisted. "What could Evangeline have known about her? She had so much. She was beautiful and young and Philip James was terribly in love with her . . ."

"No," Henrietta said. "No, you're wrong, Philip hated her."

"Hated her?" I said. "But he has been so unhappy since she died—and they were engaged."

"He blames himself for her death, I heard them the night she threatened to kill herself. We all knew Philip wasn't in love with her, but Silas wanted them to be married. Philip had always been so grateful to Silas that he agreed to do it—it probably didn't seem a difficult thing to do even though she was shallow and superficial. She was so beautiful and gay and when they became engaged that was all he knew about her."

I turned from the window and came over to Henrietta who seemed at ease now, lounging in the easy chair.

"It's beginning to make sense," I said "Silas Meredith wanted him to marry her to revenge himself on his own daughters whom he hated."

"I don't know anything about that. Silas was dying and he was very fond of Eleanor—too fond of her, we always thought, for anyone's good. And she was carrying on all the time with George."

Henrietta sat forward angrily.

"I know George doesn't love me, but he's the only thing I care about. I've waited for him for years. He never loved anyone until the Vaughn girl came along. She was his type. I saw that right away. I went to pieces when I learned he was having an affair with her. Then, just before Silas died, from the moment he was bedridden in fact, Eleanor began to go around with Philip."

"It was fortunate for you he was on the scene."

"I'm sure Eleanor's interest in Philip was purely mercenary—not that Philip isn't attractive, too, but he was too much the scholar for her. George was so jealous of Philip that he wrote her all kinds of foolish letters. Did you find any of them in your room?"

"There were some letters in the desk when I first came, but Mrs. Hawkins removed them."

"Then Hawkins lied, Evangeline must have them."

"But if Philip never loved Eleanor Vaughn why should he have come to hate her?"

"Perhaps because he found out she had been deceiving Silas. Remember .Philip feels he owes everything to Silas—especially since he was so generous in his will. Anyhow he was terribly bitter that night I overheard them—two days before she died. She pleaded with him desperately not to break with her. She flung herself on his mercy, pleaded that she loved him—it was right in this room—but he only laughed. And then she threatened to kill herself. I can still hear the way he warned her."

"Warned her? How?"

" 'If you don't watch your step,' he told her, 'someone will save you the trouble.' "

The fire crackled, and one of the logs slipped out of place. I watched Henrietta awkwardly replace it.

"I can't understand," I murmured, "what he meant by that. Did Eleanor Vaughn have enemies?"

"Of course. Anyone so mean and deceitful deserved to have enemies. What sadistic delight she always took in showing me the letters George wrote her."

"But why did she act that way? She had no reason to be jealous of you."

"Probably out of sheer vengeance. There was something about her past of which she was ashamed."

"You mean because she was illegitimate?"

"How did you know? Yes, that was one of the reasons."

"Who were her enemies?"

"Her enemies? Why, you ought to know. Her enemies are—yours. Can't you see that?"

Henrietta rose, her blue eyes very wide.

"I have said too much," she muttered.

She hurried out of the studio and down the path.

As soon as her small, squat figure was out of sight, I quickly locked the door again. My new-born hope had been overshadowed by Henrietta's last words. There was no time to lose. Henrietta had not asked to see the portrait, but the next visitor might show some curiosity.

I took the picture to the east room. In the semidarkness I studied the rows of shelves that nearly reached the ceiling. The topmost was surely an ideal hiding place.

The old studio stepladder creaked under my weight. I stood tiptoe on top of the ladder, and carefully shoved the portrait behind a stack of art supplies, out of sight. Just as I withdrew my arm the wrapping fell away from one of the packages in front, revealing a pile of brand new canvases. I was about to replace the paper when I noticed something singular: one canvas was individually wrapped. Curious to learn why this one should be more carefully preserved than the others I slowly pulled it out. My fingers closed around something hard. This was no unused canvas. It had a frame. The wrapping paper dropped to the floor. I stared at the missing Mona Lisa.

I stared hard at it. Why should anyone have gone to the trouble of concealing this picture? Why should it have been removed from the wall in the first place? As I turned the picture round I thought I found the answer. The paper backing was split across the top. And something was concealed between the canvas and the backing!

Glancing nervously toward the large windows, I reached inside the makeshift pocket and pulled out two envelopes. In the first was a notebook filled with a series of sketches. On the cover was the face of Eleanor Vaughn. But the eyes had changed. This was a tale of terror, graphically told.

On the first page, Eleanor Vaughn, her body poised for flight, sought to ward off a group of pursuers who were seeking to tear a bag of money from her hands. My lips grew dry as I stared at the group. I knew them all—Evangeline, George Mundin, and Helena were there; Cornelia, Mrs. Hawkins, Rudlow and Philip! Meredith Hall was a veritable Golgotha where Eleanor Vaughn finally grappled with the bloody figure of death. But on the last page she was triumphant, scornfully looking down at the cringing figures of her erstwhile assailants, now bound together by chains of empty money bags.

What was the message behind these sinister sketches and for whom had this message been intended?

The second envelope was addressed to Eleanor. The name of a well-known travel agency was printed on the flap. I opened it. There was nothing inside this envelope save two steamship tickets, dated December twenty-fourth—just eight days before I had arrived at Meredith Hall.

In the silent, late afternoon hush, I stole back to my room.

Envelopes and painting had been put back where I had found them. Until I had decided on a course of action it seemed sensible to leave this evidence in its hiding place.

One salient fact stood out above all others. Eleanor Vaughn had feared for her life; now she was dead. And I had wanted to take her place. I loved Philip. Even were I denied Philip's love, I would never take my own life. Such an act is the choice of a coward or a hysterical person. To the best of my knowledge Eleanor Vaughn had been neither.

If the steamship tickets had originally been intended for a honeymoon trip, why weren't they in Philip's possession and in his name? Why had they been concealed? If the second ticket were not intended for Philip, for whom was it? Would any person, fearing for her life, seek refuge in death?

Flight was more obviously indicated. Perhaps Eleanor Vaughn had been trying to escape when—when what?

Someone had stopped her!

There. That was it. Someone had prevented Eleanor Vaughn from escaping. That was the truth. Murder.

She had been murdered. Elaine must have known. That was the secret she had tried to tell me.

Did Philip also know the truth? Is that what had been torturing him all these months? And if it was, why had he kept it to himself? Whom was he shielding?

A doubt that had crept into my mind when I first saw the strange sketches assailed me again, obliterating all other thoughts.

"Oh, God," I prayed, "please let it not be Philip—please . . ."

But, I considered, there was no need for Philip to have done it. He had severed his relationship with the girl. I quickly stifled my answer to myself—"A suprisingly large sum of money . . . revert to Philip . . ." Cornelia Fiske's words had been in my mind. On the other hand —"Her enemies are yours," Henrietta had said. "Her enemies are yours." I had no money. The drawing had left no further doubt in my mind as to their identities. They were all in it. I felt completely alone. This person had been successful once, why not a second time?

Frantically I locked the door. At least it was safe within these four walls. But was it?

Suddenly I recalled a sheet of white paper with a brief salutation, "Dear Evelyn—"

This was the person to whom Eleanor Vaughn had appealed at the very last. The letter had never been written but if I could find her, this unknown Evelyn might be able to unravel the whole mystery.

Where could she be reached? Was it a man or a woman? Who would know Evelyn's whereabouts? Perhaps Mrs. Hawkins . . .

I decided to visit Mrs. Hawkins.

The hall was crowded with girls on their way to supper. I went up the narrow stairs to the third floor. All the doors above were shut, but I could hear Mrs. Hawkins moving noisily about her room.

I knocked. After a few minutes the door opened, and she stood peering at me.

"What do you want?"

"I've come about Eleanor Vaughn's belongings. Could you tell me where they were put after you removed them from my room?"

"Why do you want to know?"

"It seems that some of my correspondence became mixed up with hers."

"Hardly likely. I cleared out the room the day after you came."

"I know that, but I left a list of addresses in the desk."

"That's too bad. What do you expect me to do about it? First Miss Evangeline asking about Miss Vaughn's clothes, and now here you come and—"

"How odd of her to be interested in those clothes."

"Miss Evangeline checks up on everything. She's very methodical. The suit Miss Vaughn died in has been hanging in a paper bag all these months and it wasn't touched since I removed it from the body. 'I'm sure the law doesn't require us to preserve the suit any longer,' said Miss Evangeline, 'take the package down to Mr. James. Ask him what should be its disposition.' "

I was shocked. Evangeline knew how the sight of those garments, more than anything else, would bring back the horror of that fatal day to Philip, would make him relive those hours of torture. Was this a prelude to something more sinister? Or was it a threat?

"Even the bloodstains were still on the clothes, Miss Hunter," continued Mrs. Hawkins, "but they wouldn't be hard to wash away. Even the coroner admired the suit."

"The coroner! What did he have to do with this?"

"Autopsy. There had to be an autopsy—to determine the immediate cause of death. But when they learned about her and Mr. Philip no longer being engaged, the coroner said it was suicide because of a broken heart."

I followed her down the passage to a tall clothes press in the rear. After fumbling with the ring of keys which always hung from her belt, she found the right one. In a few seconds I was looking at the same wardrobe I had found in my room that first night. My eyes swept past the carefully hung garments to the boxes and pieces of luggage on the shelf. I reached toward them, and then hesitated, casting an inquiring glance toward Mrs. Hawkins.

"May I look through those?"

"Go on," she said sharply, "but don't take your time about it."

I made a rapid search. There were no letters.

"Come along now," said Mrs. Hawkins impatiently. "I can't waste any more time."

This then was defeat, hopeless defeat. Then, acting on impulse, I turned to the house mother.

"Do you remember Evelyn?" I asked eagerly.

I saw her jaw sag, and her eyes rolled back until the whites of them showed prominently.

"She's not coming back," she cried. "Don't you try any of the Vaughn girl's tricks. Evelyn is never coming back!"

At that moment I realized I had blundered. Mrs. Hawkins was linked with my enemies. Unwittingly, I had played into her hands. I turned and fled.

The second-floor corridor was deserted. As I moved toward my room I could hear voices and the familiar rattle of dishes coming up from the dining hall. I had no appetite for food, nor did I dare explain my late arrival to Evangeline. Her trusted servant would tell her all about it soon enough.

I opened my door. Seated on a chair by the window, nonchalantly smoking a cigarette, was George Mundin!

"What is the meaning of this?" I demanded. "What are you doing in my room?"

"Waiting for you. You were so deucedly long in coming that I thought possibly Hawkins had done you in."

"I don't think you're funny. Please go at once!"

"Not until I get what I came for, or have you hidden them away?"

"I don't know what you mean."

"No?" He rose lazily to his feet. "Come on, now, my sweet. I want a look at those papers I saw you poring over in the studio this afternoon. Unfortunately Porter came along. It wouldn't do to have him think me a Peeping Tom, what? I had to move along."

"How dare you spy on me?"

"I always spy on beautiful women. When a man feels his back is to the wall, he will do almost anything."

"I don't understand what you're talking about."

"My dear child, in common parlance, Evangeline is about to spring the trap. I am too lazy to take to my heels, but I would feel more comfortable if I could lay my hands on two particular letters."

"Did you write only two? What a lover!"

"These were not a lover's letters—or," he added slowly, "perhaps they were at that."

"Why are they so important to you?"

"You wouldn't want Evangeline to get hold of threatening notes you had written, now would you?"

Was this a confession? He came toward me, and his hands closed on my shoulders.

"You look so much like her," he whispered huskily. "You're driving me crazy, the way she did."

"Leave me alone . . . let go of me!"

He forced his arms about me.

"If—if you will meet me at the studio tomorrow morning," I promised in desperation, "I'll show you what I found."

"Make it tonight," he urged, holding me tight. "After the others retire. We have a good excuse for going there together now."

"Get out of here! Get out of here, and don't you dare come near me again!"

His attitude changed. He released me abruptly, and slyly looking at me said, "No man likes to be spurned by a woman. The coroner would be interested to learn about the special clause in Silas Meredith's will."

"What special clause?"

"Don't tell me you didn't know the money the old man bequeathed to Eleanor was to go to Philip James in the event her death antedated his! Just bear that in mind, won't you? Cheerio until tomorrow morning."

Hardly had Mundin left me when the door was flung open, and Henrietta stood on the threshold, her eyes blazing, and her whole small dumpy figure quivering.

"You hypocrite," she shrilled, "I saw George come out of your room. To think you were secretly laughing at me in the studio, when all the time I thought you had my interests at heart."

"Please believe me, I have. It was not—not what you think—"

I never finished the sentence, for, swooping down on me, she cut in, "I wondered where you were during supper. I came here because I thought you were ill, you—you—"

"Henrietta, believe me. I didn't know George was in my room. He was here when I returned."

"You're no better than she was. Be careful that you don't meet the same end."

"I'm not afraid," I answered. "I'm not afraid."

She ran from me. I could hear her pattering down the corridor.

Mary found me standing in the place Henrietta had left me, when she arrived with a tray of food.

"Mother of God," she exclaimed, setting the tray on the desk, "what's come over you, child? What are you starin' at so?"

"It's not easy to explain, Mary. It's only that, well, there are so many things going on here that I don't understand.'

"Don't try."

"But I must, Mary." Then I heard myself saying, "Did you ever hear Miss Vaughn speak of anyone named Evelyn?"

Her reaction to this question was even stranger than Mrs. Hawkins'. She turned up the bed lamp silently, and then crossed to the windows. Wordlessly she flung them wide open.

"Mary," I pleaded, "you do know. I can see you do. Please tell me. Who is Evelyn? Where can I find her?"

"Don't ask me . . . don't ask me that. Anything else, but please not that!"

"Please, Mary. You say you want to help me. This may be your only chance. Who was Evelyn?"

She looked furtively toward the door, and then back to me.

"Evelyn used to work here. She was the housekeeper until her mind was took, and they put her in the Rudlow Sanitarium."

Chapter XVIII

MRS. WILSEY'S Evvie and this Evelyn were the same person. Mrs. Wilsey had said her aunt was sane—that fitted into the scheme of things. Evelyn knew too much. It had been unsafe to allow her to remain at the school.

I had to talk to Evelyn. Mrs. Wilsey could be relied upon to arrange that meeting. In the meantime I wanted to question Diana. There must have been some connection between Eleanor and Rudlow.

Early next morning I brought Diana to my room.

"Diana," I began, "you said once that you might be able to help me. Would you mind telling me something about Eleanor Vaughn?"

"What?" she asked warily.

"When you parted, did she tell you that she planned to go to South America?"

"I'm not going to talk. I won't get into trouble."

"Whatever you tell me, Diana, will go no further. You ought to know that. I haven't betrayed your confidence in the past."

Diana was thoughtful for a moment. Then she began to talk.

"The night Mr. James broke off with Eleanor, she came to me. She was frightened. I'd never seen her that way before. She said she had to go away, but I wasn't so surprised because Eleanor always did unexpected things—that was part of what made her so fascinating. I asked her to take me along. She knew how I hated it here. Even though Eleanor was a good deal older than I, we always enjoyed being together. I couldn't think of staying on without her. Eleanor went to the city the very next day and came back with the steamship tickets. We were going to sail the following evening. We were both so excited when we made our plans. It was going to be so simple. We were to go to the city separately and meet at her bank. I waited there for her for hours, until the bank closed. I was frantic by then, and finally I had to call up the school."

"You know it wasn't an accident," I said distinctly.

"I don't know! I don't know anything. Eleanor's dead. I can't help her any more. I have to think of myself. I don't want to get involved. Look what happened to Elaine!"

"All right, Diana, let's forget about what I just said. Only tell me one more thing. Did Eleanor Vaughn ever speak to you of Doctor Rudlow?"

"She couldn't stand him!"

"Was there a reason?"

"Perhaps there was. She'd known him a long time. They met abroad. When Eleanor came to the United States to live and went to art school in Philadelphia—"

"Philadelphia?"

"Yes. Didn't you know he once ran a sanitarium in Germantown?"

"Why do you suppose," I wondered aloud, "he gave up a sanitarium there to come to a small town like Seacliffe?"

"Because of Eleanor. He was madly in love with her in those days."

But after Diana had gone I had no more time to ponder this strange information. The important thing was the steamship tickets which were indisputably my sole piece of concrete evidence. I hurried down to the studio where I had left them the day before.

Before going inside I looked carefully down the path to see whether George Mundin was on his way to take advantage of the offer I had so rashly made.

It was dark in the east room. When I turned on the light there, on the wall, in place of the Matisse, hung the Mona Lisa.

With shaking hands I lifted the picture down. A new backing had been put on it. I tore through the paper and peered inside. Both the folder and tickets were gone. I rushed to the closet. On the top shelf I found the Matisse. Someone—it had to be the murderer—or an accomplice—had hurried down to the studio ahead of me.

Whoever was guilty was now on guard. I, not the killer, was being trailed, and I had received due warning. But I had another reliable source for evidence.

I hurried back to the main house to phone Mrs. Wilsey. At this hour Philip had a class, so I used the phone in his office.

"This is Nancy Hunter," I told Mrs. Wilsey. "Can you meet me in town tonight?"

"Don't mind if I do."

"Good. Let's meet at the drugstore at eight o'clock?"

I distinctly heard two clicks after Mrs. Wilsey had rung off. There was only one other extension, and that was in Evangeline's room.

As I replaced the receiver, I noticed something in the bottom of Philip's wastebasket. It was the torn pieces of the last sketch in the notebook I had found in the studio the previous day.

I heard the doorknob turn, and Philip called, "Open the door. Who's in there?"

"It's I, Nancy."

I stuffed the torn sketch into my bag and let him in.

"What are you doing locked in my office?"

"Philip," I said without preamble, "I have something to tell you. Something shocking, something appalling."

"What is it?"

And then I told him. I said it so matter-of-factly, I hardly understood my composure.

"Philip, Eleanor Vaughn didn't kill herself. She was murdered."

"You must be mad!"

I went on to explain about the discovery of the tickets in the studio. I omitted all references to Evelyn and to my own immediate danger, trying to focus his attention on the fact that Eleanor had met a violent death by an unknown hand.

"If what you say is true—it's too ghastly to contemplate!" Philip exclaimed. "Murder! But why?"

"That's what I've been asking myself, and that's what I have to find out."

"No. You must forget what you've learned, forget all about it, do you hear?"

His hand gripped my shoulder until it hurt.

"Philip, I can't. Don't you see that I can't. No matter what comes of it, I have to go on. I can't stop. Philip. Look," I fumbled in my bag until I had collected all the bits of paper. Then I pieced them together on the blotter. "I found this in your wastebasket. Someone knows how much I have discovered, and—"

"Good God!" he broke in. "Did she think I had a grudge against her? Why should I—"

"You must see the implications of this, Philip. The person who has been watching me planted the sketch where it would look as though you had destroyed it. This murderer is very clever."

"What a thing to happen to Evangeline!"

"Why are you thinking of her?"

"Don't you see what this means? If everything you say is true, and there is a murderer here, Meredith Hall is finished. And if—if what you say is correct, then I was not responsible for Eleanor's death!"

"I know, Philip, but we have to prove it. If we don't apprehend the murderer, you will be in danger. You must see that someone is trying to make you appear guilty. It is all so well planned that if I go ahead and prove without doubt that there has been a murder committed you will be suspected."

"I don't understand. Why should anyone do this to me?"

"Many crimes have been committed because of money. Aren't you depriving the Merediths of some of the fortune they might otherwise have inherited?"

"I never thought of it that way. Silas was my stepfather. I was devoted to him."

"If only Silas Meredith had not stipulated that all the money he left Eleanor was to pass on to you in the event she died before you."

"I never touched that money, Nancy. I don't want any part of it. I told Evangeline to use it for the school."

"Did you? Is that in writing?"

"In writing? No, of course not. Between brother and sister—"

"Oh, Philip, if that matter came up in court and you couldn't show proof that you offered the money to Evangeline, they would condemn you for that."

"But Evangeline would tell the truth. They would have to believe her. I'm going to Evangeline right now. It wouldn't be fair to act without her knowledge."

"No, Philip, no! You mustn't do that. Don't tell Evangeline!"

"Why not? Surely you don't suspect her!"

"There has been a murder. Everyone is suspect now."

Philip paced up and down the room. "I have to think this over. Do nothing further. Please wait until I speak to you again."

There were only three of us riding down on the bus that night—Helena, Mrs. Hawkins and I. It was a dismal, silent journey.

Left to my own gloomy thoughts, doubt as to the prudence of this excursion began to assail me. Was I not placing too much confidence in Mrs. Wilsey. And what would Philip say to my deliberate flouting of his orders? Thoughts of Philip brought a wave of fresh uneasiness. I had not seen him since morning. He was said to have gone off somewhere with Evangeline—to dinner at the home of one of the wealthier day students. I prayed desperately that he would not confide in her.

As we neared the village, the driver turned around and inquired where the first stop would be.

"Miss Helena," Mrs. Hawkins asked, "are we going to the shoemaker's first?"

Helena stirred, as though roused from a deep reverie.

"Yes, yes, of course. Those were my instructions. Why can't any of you remember what you are told?"

My companions were not interested in my destination.

"I will be ready to return with you at nine-thirty," I told Helena.

"Very well," she said, " meet us in front of the post office."

I left them and walked down the quiet street. Mrs. Wilsey had already arrived at the pharmacy. We seated ourselves in one of the booths and gave our order to the young soda clerk.

"You sounded kind of cautious-like this morning." Mrs. Wilsey said. "What's on your mind, girl?"

"Ever since I saw you, I've been thinking of what you told me about Evvie."

"Are you coming to that place with me?"

"Yes, I am. I want to meet Evvie. I must find out for myself if she is really normal. For, if she is—" I paused because I had to choose my words, "we will have to appeal to the proper authorities. How soon do you think we can visit her?"

"Well, now, you're playing in luck. After I spoke to you this morning, I had an idea you would want to see her, so I called the sanitarium right away for an appointment. Doctor Rudlow hemmed and hawed, said something about not allowing visitors too often because it excited the patients. 'Listen, Doctor,' I says. 'Evvie needs cheering. I can come and bring her some of my old-fashioned strawberry shortcake. She was right fond of that in the old days.' Well, he fell for that talk, hook, line and sinker. 'You may come tomorrow,' he says, 'at three o'clock. And leave a piece of that cake for me.' "

She paused for a moment to allow the clerk to serve us. As soon as he was out of hearing she bent forward again.

"On Saturday afternoons Doctor Rudlow goes to the city with Miss Evangeline. I've seen them often. So we can have a long chat with Evvie. You meet me there right in front of the building. We'll go in together. No one will know you from Eve, my daughter, there, and I can say you're my girl. Not that that's a compliment to you."

It was only eight-thirty when we had concluded our arrangements, and the bus was not due for another hour. Unfortunately, my companion did not have her car.

"Why don't we go to the movies for a while?" I suggested. "It's too nasty out for walking."

Mrs. Wilsey thought this was a good idea, and we went.

At nine-thirty there was still no sign of the bus. There was a thick fog, and the night was black. The street in front of the post office was deserted, and it soon appeared that Mrs. Wilsey and I were the only two people in Seacliffe at that hour.

"Let's find Jeggy Williams. He'll drive us back," I suggested after we had paced up and down, vainly looking for the bus.

"Jeggy's not around tonight. He's on a job up at Dead Man's Cove. Guess we'll have to walk," said Mrs. Wilsey cheerfully. "Won't be the first time for me. Standing here in this dampness ain't going to help my rheumatics any."

After I had left Mrs. Wilsey, the unpleasant part of my journey began. I turned off the highway and trudged up the ascending road to the school.

Setting one foot carefully before the other, I made my way to the school gate. I assumed that Mrs. Hawkins and Helena must still be out and wondered if I had done wrong in not waiting for them longer. But I had waited. It had been after ten when we left the village.

The main building loomed up darkly. Now, more than ever, I was convinced there was a streak of insanity in every one of the Merediths, not enough to make it apparent to the casual observer, but enough to make them dangerous.

The upper passage was still. Not a sound came from the dormitories as I stole across the carpet to my room. As had been my habit of late, I entered the room and turned on the floor lamp before closing the door.

I took the key from my bag, set it in the lock and turned it. There was no customary, reassuring click. I withdrew the key and stared at it. It looked like the one that belonged to the room, but was it? Someone might have deliberately exchanged this key for the one I always carried in my bag. But perhaps the lock was only broken.

I undressed and prepared for bed as though nothing had occurred. I collected paper and pencil, for I wanted to make notes on what had happened during the day. Then I turned on the bed lamp. The light was dim. Something seemed to be wrong with the bulb. It flickered and wavered, flickered and wavered. Writing under such a poor light was a strain on my eyes. I was, moreover, too restless to concentrate. Unable to shake off a growing panic, I climbed out of bed, turned off the floor lamp, and went to open the windows. After a few attempts I noticed that the cords of both windows were broken. I had expected this to happen any day because the cords were so old and worn, but I couldn't help wondering whether it was not something that had been deliberately planned.

I looked at my watch. It was just twelve-fifteen. I settled myself in bed once more and forced my eyes to follow the text of a novel. I frowned impatiently at the flickering electric bulb. Suddenly it flickered out. Darkness entombed me.

Eleanor Vaughn haunted me as the minutes dragged by. Whose hand had reached out to push her over the side of the cliff? Whose?

All at once I caught the sound that I had subconsciously been waiting for. There were faint footfalls outside my door. Tensely I waited, my body paralyzed. The door was opening. I heard muffled breathing. A dark shadow stood among the shadows at the far end of the room. A shapeless shadow, an obscure shadow.

The counterpane rippled over my body. Someone was touching the pillows next to my head. That motion, that barely perceptible contact released me, and I leaped out of bed on the side away from the prowler.

There was a swift movement. The door opened and closed almost at once with a bang. I lost a moment trying to get to the floor lamp. The faint light hurt my eyes.

I rushed out into the corridor. There was no one in sight. All the doors were closed. I tried to remember which was Philip's room. Mary had told me once, but now I was not sure.

Sudden light blinded my eyes. I had not heard a door open. Evangeline stood on the threshold of her room.

"Miss Hunter, what's wrong? You look insane."'

"I'm sorry," I stammered. "I was so frightened. I didn't mean to disturb you."

"Of course not. Poor child. So it was your door that slammed. I'm a very light sleeper, and the least sound disturbs me."

"I didn't bang my door. Someone else—"

"Poor child. We must not wake the others. You have had a bad dream. But you're safe now. No one is going to hurt you."

She took me gently but firmly by the arm and led me into her room.

"But you don't understand. Someone came to my room—"

"There, there," she said, pressing me into the chair by her dressing table. "Don't talk. Just relax. I'll find something to cover your shoulders before you catch cold. Then we'll go back to your room together."

"You don't understand," I repeated hysterically. "Someone tried to smother me!"

She did not say anything, but I saw her deftly remove the nail file and scissors from the table. The realization brought home by this act calmed me instantly. Evangeline's manner was kindliness itself, but she was behaving just as though I were really insane and had to be humored.

Silently she helped me into a robe, and then she handed me a pair of mules.

"Now tell me all about your dream," she said, sitting on the arm of my chair, her arm around my shoulders.

"It wasn't a dream," I protested, shrinking away from her body. "Someone deliberately planned to kill me."

Her fingers pressed into my shoulder.

"Go on," she urged, "someone was trying to kill you, and then you woke up."

This last was said almost playfully, and roused my anger.

"You don't believe me," I said quietly. "Well, come to my room. I'll show you how the lock has been tampered with or else my key was exchanged for another."

Then I mentioned the broken window cords.

"Oh, of course," Evangeline said, "Hawkins spoke of them this morning. They broke while the window cleaner was here."

"Come to my room, and I'll show you the key doesn't work."

She led the way down the passage to my room. On the threshold she paused. I had left the key in the lock. She turned it swiftly. There was a familiar click. There was nothing wrong with the lock or key.

"Perhaps I had better send for Doctor Rudlow," said Evangeline.

"No, no! Don't send for him. I'm all right." But a flood of self-doubt engulfed me. Was I losing my reason? Other people had gone mad from too much stress and strain.

"Perhaps I did imagine that someone came here to harm me," I said helplessly. "Maybe I was only dreaming—"

"Of course. You had a nightmare and mistook it for reality. Do you have such delusions often? Well, never mind," she hastened to add, "we won't discuss that now." She said carefully, "This is something you would not want anyone to hear of. I will keep your secret."

She left the room. I wanted to call her back again. I was afraid to be alone. And then I saw a small metal object glittering on the carpet.

Mechanically I stooped to pick it up. For several minutes my eyes clung to the key in the palm of my hand and then to the key in the lock. Then I began to laugh. Anyone seeing me then would surely have doubted my sanity. But in this unexpected outburst of mirth there was relief, great relief.

Chapter XIX

J EGGY CALLED for me the next day at half past two. Until his arrival I had been on tenterhooks for fear something would go wrong, but apparently no one intended to checkmate my plans. Evangeline had chosen to go to the city on that bright April day and for all I knew, Philip had gone along. I saw him only for a brief moment at breakfast, and he had seemed anxious to avoid seeing me alone. Since I had a guilty conscience myself, I was just as happy to keep out of his way.

While not allowing my thoughts to dwell on the ghastly experience of the previous night, I could not help but ponder Evangeline's intentions. Would she insist on my seeing Rudlow, or would she keep silent as she had promised?

Of one thing I was certain. I dared not spend another night at Meredith Hall.

Jeggy met me at the gate.

"Where to?" he asked cheerfully, as the shabby-looking car coursed down the hill.

"The Rudlow Sanitarium. I'm going to meet Mrs. Wilsey there."

"That so! Funny. I saw her this morning, but she didn't say she had a date with you."

"Does she always tell you where she is going?"

"Most times she does. Mrs. Wilsey is a great one for jawing a bit now and then y'know. Guess it slipped her mind."

The sanitarium was just five miles out of Seacliffe. Rudlow had purchased an old mansion that stood on some forty-three acres of rolling country. Dense woods bordered it on two sides, and a high stone wall marked off the rest of the property.

Jeggy did not stop the car immediately in front of the entrance, because I didn't want to go inside without Mrs. Wilsey. The doorman, who looked like a former wrestler, eyed us with unconcern, as though it was not unusual for a strange car to come and park near the house.

A quarter of an hour passed. What could be detaining the woman? Suppose, I thought apprehensively, Doctor Rudlow had not gone to the city, but was merely out on a call. He might return at any moment. Then it would be all over.

"Jeggy," I said determinedly, "I'm going ahead. Please tell Mrs. Wilsey to meet me inside." I hesitated for an instant, and then decided to be franker with the man. "I am going to visit her Aunt Evvie."

"You're gonna visit a crazy woman, Miss Hunter! My, you're brave!"

I laughed briefly. "Mrs. Wilsey's aunt is not—not dangerous. Nothing is going to happen to me. If it does," I added flippantly, "just notify the folks back home."

The doorman stared at me owlishly. He escorted me inside and left me at a desk in the corridor behind which was seated an oldish woman in nurse's uniform.

"Register there," she commanded. "Name. Address."

"But I'm not a patient," I protested.

"You might be sometime. You look the nervous type."

"I—I—have an appointment with Miss Perkins."

"There, you see," the nurse said triumphantly. "You are the nervous type. I can spot all of you in an instant. What you need is a few weeks here under the vigilance of Doctor Rudlow. He would cure you."

"You have faith in him . . ." I said, to make conversation.

"I was head nurse at his first sanitarium. That goes pretty far back, I guess. In fact," proudly, "I was the first patient he ever psychoanalyzed."

My interest quickened.

"That must have been quite an ordeal. I suppose Doctor Rudlow has psychoanalyzed many other people since then."

My eagerness must have been too apparent, for the nurse suddenly snapped back into her shell.

"Whom did you say you came to visit?" she asked.

"Mrs. Wilsey's Aunt Evvie," I fumbled, "Miss Perkins."

She looked up at her calender. "That's right. Mrs. Wilsey is expected. But who are you?"

"I'm—I'm another Miss Perkins—her niece—"

"Of course. I recognized you from the picture she has in her room. Come along." Suddenly she stopped short. "But that girl in the picture —she's dead!" Her face turned the color of her uniform. "My God," she gasped, "maybe Perkins really is—" She broke off abruptly and eyed me with suspicion. "Who are you really?"

"I've already told you—Evelyn's niece. Of course, there is a resemblance between the girl in the picture and me, but I'm not that person. We—we just look alike, that's all."

Still looking unconvinced the woman led me down the hall to a sitting room.

"You'll have to wait here until the doctor comes back," she said.

If she expected me to wait, Rudlow could not have gone to the city.

"But you don't understand," I cried, suddenly fearful. "The longer I wait, the less time I'll have to spend with my aunt."

"I have my orders. No visitors are allowed to see the patients without Doctor Rudlow's approval."

"But he gave Mrs. Wilsey permission."

"Yes," she seemed to be weakening, "but she didn't mention that you were coming."

"She probably didn't think it necessary. Why do you have to take such precautions? Are the majority of the patients here mental cases?"

"Oh, no. But our patients have faith in the doctor's theory that sickness originates in the mind. Doctor Rudlow subjects his patients to a series of mental treatments in order to get at the root of their difficulties."

"He's fortunate to have a loyal person like you in his employ."

She looked pleased.

It seemed unlikely that the nurse could be bribed, and yet . . . I opened my pocketbook with feigned nonchalance and caught a flash in her eyes.

"It must grow dull for you sometimes. Doctor Rudlow is away from the sanitarium a good deal. Of course, there are other nurses—"

"Not many. I handle anything of importance that the doctor hasn't time for himself."

I drew a five-dollar bill out and mentally kissed it good-by.

"It looks as though Mrs. Wilsey isn't coming," I said, "and there doesn't seem to be much use in my waiting around for the doctor. He generally goes to the city on Saturdays, my aunt says, with the Headmistress from the Hall."

The arrow struck home. I saw the change of expression on the woman's face. It wasn't loyalty alone that kept her here after all. Taking my cue, I slipped the money into her willing hand.

"Tell Aunt Evelyn I asked after her, won't you?"

A few seconds later I was following the nurse up an enclosed staircase. At frequent intervals we would pass through a door which had to be unlocked. The nurse carefully locked it again behind me.

At last we reached what I judged to be the fourth floor of the house and stepped into a wide passage. The nurse unlocked one of the many closed doors and admitted me into a plain, simply furnished room. The windows were barred.

A woman sat in a rocker sewing. She scarcely lifted her head and greeted the nurse in a listless voice.

I should have recognized Evelyn anywhere as being related to Mrs. Wilsey and the seamstress. The same bone structure prevailed in her face, the same prominent nose with its receding nostrils.

As her glance shifted from the nurse to me a change came over the woman. A hoarse cry broke from her lips, "Eleanor!" She half rose from her seat, her arms flung out. Then brushing her hands across her eyes, as if to dispel a picture, she sank back into the chair with a low moan.

"Merciful God!" she muttered. "The doctor's right. I am out of my senses."

The nurse looked at me queerly, and I knew now was the time to put on the performance of my life.

"Aunt Evvie," I cried, rushing toward the woman. "Don't you know me? I'm Isabel. Your own sister's child."

She continued to stare incredulously.

"You must remember me, Aunt Evvie. I was the one who looked like Eleanor."

"You sweet child," she said, "to think of you coming to see your aunt. I—I haven't forgotten you. I—I—"

The nurse was satisfied. She prepared to leave.

"You may stay here fifteen minutes," she told me.

I heard the door close, and the key turned in the lock. I was alone with Evelyn at last.

Almost unconsciously I backed away toward the door.

"What is it?" Evelyn said. "Don't be afraid. I'm quite well. Tell me who you are, and why you have come here."

These questions were so natural that I felt less timid.

"I was to have come here with your niece, Mrs. Wilsey," I explained. "I don't know what happened to her. We want to help you get out of here."

"They'll never let me go," Evelyn said. "I know too much. The Lord knows I wouldn't talk if they let me out. Why should I? He's dead, and she's dead. Nothing can bring them back."

"Whom do you mean?" I asked in wonderment. "Eleanor Vaughn and who else?"

She did not answer.

I knelt at her feet. "Miss Perkins, I've come to see you because you were the last person Eleanor Vaughn appealed to before she died."

"Is that true? Are you really telling me the truth?"

Tears coursed down her cheeks.

"Yes. She had begun a letter to you— It was on the desk—"

"Where is it? Did you bring it with you? Let me have it."

"I'm sorry. I don't have it with me. You see she had only written the salutation."

Evelyn closed her eyes, and sat back.

"Miss Perkins," I said gently, "we have so little time. Won't you help me? You see, I've made some discoveries—" I spoke hesitantly for I didn't want to add to her suffering. "I have reason to believe Eleanor was murdered."

I saw her shrink from me, her whole body crumpling.

"No, no, no, no," she kept repeating the word.

At last she said, "I thought of that when they first told me she was dead, but I wouldn't let myself believe it. Of course, it's true! It had to end that way. I was afraid for her. Eleanor wouldn't have hurt anyone, not deliberately, I mean. She was thoughtless—but all young people are today. It was bad company that ruined her. First Rudlow, he took her money. I begged her to stay away from him, but she would not litsen."

I was bewildered. Why should Eleanor Vaughn have obeyed a servant?

As if reading my mind, she said slowly, "Eleanor Vaughn was my daughter."

"Your daughter!"

"Yes. She never had a fair chance like other girls. Eleanor never knew who her father was until she was grown up. No one here ever guessed. Things would have been different if Silas hadn't told Evangeline just before he passed away. That started all the real trouble."

"You can't mean that Silas Meredith was Eleanor's father!"

"The Merediths are a bad lot, but my child would have been different if they had let her alone. We would never have come back to Meredith Hall if it hadn't been for Emile and the money. I wish to God we had stayed away."

"How long have you known Rudlow?"

"Eleanor met him at some kind of faith-healers' gathering when we were still living in England. He had just finished studying medicine in Vienna. When he sailed for America, he persuaded Eleanor to follow him and I had to come along. I didn't like the looks of things, but he had her so bewitched she wouldn't listen to reason. She said she wanted to go to art school in this country. At the time I thought she had real talent, and I hoped the work would take her mind off the doctor."

She sighed. "You're probably wondering about Silas and me. Sometimes a woman can't help loving the wrong man. After the first Mrs. Meredith had borne him two daughters, Silas learned she could not have another child. He grew bitter. He felt he had been cheated by life because he didn't have a son, but he could not divorce his wife for fear the scandal would ruin the school. It was a boys' school in those days you know. I was pretty in those days. He soon found out that I was in love with him—he was so handsome. He began seeing a lot of me. He used to say that if it was all right in Biblical times for a man with a barren wife to have a child by his handmaiden, it was for him, too. He was a great churchgoer. When he found out that I was going to have a baby he sent me away. I lived like a queen during those months. Then when I had a daughter he was furious. I went to England with my baby. Then I heard Mrs. Meredith had committed suicide. For years, I didn't hear from him —even though he had cared for me, in his fashion. He sent me money for a while, and then that stopped. He married a widow with a son. I wondered at the time how Evangeline took to that. She was always so jealous of her father.

"When Eleanor grew up I wanted her to have the things she was entitled to, so I wrote Silas. He sent me a large check, but told me not to bother him any more. We could have gotten along nicely on what we had, if it hadn't been for Rudlow. He was always hard up. He told Ellie that they couldn't get married unless there was more money. He had big ideas for himself. The minute we got to America, the girl was after me to write her father. She didn't know who he was, but she knew he was wealthy.

"God, how I wish that letter had never been written. I tried to put off sending it, but she gave me no peace. I was a fool to enclose a picture of Eleanor. Silas fell for the girl's looks and surprised us one day by a visit. What a shock it was to see him there after all those years. He agreed to help us, provided that we would never tell anyone the truth about Ellie. I returned to the Hall as housekeeper. His second wife had died without bearing him a child, and he said he was lonely and that it would make him happy to have Ellie and me near him. Then the Meredith in her came to the front. She used her father's fondness for her to good advantage, wheedling more and more money out of him all the time. He got rid of the art teacher so that Ellie could work at the school, too.

"Then the girl went and told Rudlow all about herself, in a bragging way, of course. That's all that crook needed. He began blackmailing Silas. He threatened to broadcast the story. So Silas set the doctor up in an office in Seacliffe. That didn't last either. He had to have a sanitarium with hospital equipment—a lot he knows about hospitals!"

"What did Evangeline say to all this?"

"She was in a rage because her father engaged Eleanor without consulting her. She was already Headmistress. Silas was amused at this. Evangeline still had no idea that Ellie was my daughter. He pitted the sisters against each other. He always had tormented Evangeline because she wasn't a boy. Funny, instead of her hating him, she adored him all the more.

"You know, Rudlow became interested in Evangeline right away. I guess he figured that since she was the eldest, she would inherit most of the money. Evangeline didn't have much time for him then. She was too busy worrying about her father and Ellie, afraid the old man would marry a young girl in his dotage."

"How do you know about this?"

"Well, strangely enough, Evangeline came to me. She thought she was hurting me by telling me of Silas' new affair. She'd remembered me all those years—she had good cause to. Later, when she learned the truth, I thought she'd kill me.

"Anyway, Eleanor grew impatient when she saw that she might not have all the position and power she wanted. Even though Silas was crazy about the girl he would never recognize her in public as his own flesh and blood for fear of hurting the family name, particularly his branch of the family. He never thought much of George's mother.

"Ellie began to blame me for everything. She was right—but it was too late for regrets. I tried to make her look at it like that, but I only made things worse. My own daughter acted like she was ashamed of me. She stopped coming to me with her troubles. She would stay away days at a time. She had other ideas up her sleeve, and played up to the students and faculty for all she was worth, hoping someday to take Evangeline's place as Headmistress. She might have succeeded if Silas hadn't died so soon.

"Her going with Philip James was another mistake. Rudlow wasn't ready to be left out of the picture entirely. He wasn't sure of how he stood with Evangeline, I guess. Perhaps he was afraid Ellie would tell Evangeline about his past."

"Then Rudlow, too, was better off after Eleanor's death?"

"Oh, sure. Most of them were. I think he was the one who first talked against Ellie to Evangeline. Ellie always spoke too freely. I can just about guess what must have happened, knowing them all like I do. After Silas had his last stroke, he changed—for the better, I mean. He was sorry for all the wrong he did. Well, I nursed him to the end because I still loved him. I was the only one he wanted near him. He didn't trust the others. Would you believe it, he wanted to marry me then. I had all I could do to convince him it was too late."

"Why didn't you marry him? Were you sure he wouldn't recover?"

"It wasn't that. I didn't see how it would improve things. Besides, I was sure Ellie helped put the idea in his head. Lord, she never forgave me for not marrying him. It would have made things easier for her in one way if I had, but you should have seen Evangeline when her father told her Ellie was our child. It took her down a peg or two when she found out Eleanor was her half-sister.

"I'm not trying to put on airs, mind you. I know I don't have their education, but if I'd had half a chance—Silas and Evangeline discussed his will that day. His lawyer had been there in the morning. Evangeline didn't let her father see how furious she was, and she promised him she would always look after Ellie and me. She wanted our names left out of the will. But Silas didn't trust his daughter. Then, well I suppose you know about the will—his leaving all that money for Ellie. He did agree to leave me out of the will and he gave me enough money to be comfortable right then. Yes. Silas must have cared for me. He was so generous at the end. But he was good to all of them, especially Philip. He thought the world of him. He couldn't have felt closer to a son. I can still hear him urging Philip and Ellie to marry. 'Your children,' he said, 'will someday inherit the whole Meredith fortune.'

"Philip is a fine man, but Ellie wasn't for him. She understood men—"

I listened to the rest of the sordid tale, hardly mindful of my surroundings. Eleanor had been paying Rudlow, who threatened to expose her to Philip. Evangeline taunted Eleanor for being the daughter of a common house servant, and turned the girl more and more against her mother. In the end Eleanor fell willingly into Evangeline's plan to remove Evelyn to an asylum. When she reached this point of the story the woman began to cry softly. I could see how this, more than any other incident, had broken her spirit.

"Are you sure Eleanor was a party to that?" I asked.

"Oh, yes. I know. You see, Rudlow wanted me here. I heard them all discussing it one night. I know why the doctor needed me. He thought someday he might blackmail Evangeline. He saw how changeable the Merediths were and wasn't so sure of her regard for him. I am a necessary witness.

"Poor Ellie. I could see even before I was taken away that she was dreaming of herself as the ruler of the family. She was so beautiful that last time I saw her. I had red hair too, until I came here. It turned white overnight, you might say. Funny, isn't it? But I don't mind about that either. If only Ellie had listened to me, Miss Hunter. But she wouldn't, because she had always made out all right doing things to suit herself."

"Why should Evangeline hate you so?" I asked.

"If Evangeline hadn't known the truth about me, I wouldn't be here. It wasn't the money in my case. Don't you know, didn't anyone ever tell you how jealous Evangeline was of her own mother? I shouldn't say this, but—it's God's truth, Miss Hunter. After I left Meredith Hall she had a dreadful argument with her mother and she told her about Silas and me. Evangeline was too young to know about the baby of course, but she made it her business to spy on people even then. That's why Deborah Meredith killed herself. Deborah loved Silas and it must have destroyed her final faith in everything."

Just then the key turned in the lock. We both gave a start, and I was jerked back to the immediate danger.

"Here's the nurse," I whispered. "I'll have to leave now, but I'm going to help you get out of this place."

The door opened, and noting a startled expression on Evelyn's face, I turned. Evangeline walked into the room.

She said, "You have been enjoying a pleasant visit. I trust I am not disturbing you."

Miss Perkins said nothing. Evangeline spoke to me.

"You have been very clever, but not clever enough."

She smiled triumphantly. Then she turned to my companion.

"And you, Evelyn, I suppose you have been sniveling about your troubles and weeping over the death of your good-for-nothing daughter."

Evelyn half rose from the seat, her face taut, her hands clenching the arms of the chair.

"You devil," she shrieked, "who are you to criticize her ways? Someday you'll pay for all your evil doings, and I hope I'm still alive to gloat. Only your father saw through you," she panted. "Silas hated you—"

Before the woman had completed her sentence, Evangeline struck her across the lips. I stood there transfixed as Evangeline looked down at Evelyn, cowering in the chair.

I began to sob hysterically, trying to fight against a feeling of helplessness this woman's presence inculcated in me.

"Doctor Rudlow is quite right," Evangeline said to me. "You are tired. You need a rest, a long rest. Perhaps in that new sanitarium Doctor Rudlow is opening in South America. I think I will have you remain right here in the meantime. I will announce tonight at supper that due to the ill health of your Cousin Julian you were unexpectedly called home."

"You can't keep me here. You'll never get away with that. Besides," I added desperately as Evangeline looked significantly toward Evelyn, "Jeggy Williams is outside waiting for me."

"I told him I would take you home. I notified Mrs. Wilsey this morning that you could not keep your appointment for today. It is too bad that women like that must gossip. Miss Perkins, our seamstress, unwittingly informed Hawkins of your intended visit."

"But you can't keep me here against my will! I'm not mad."

"But you will be, my dear."

Evangeline opened the door.

Doctor Rudlow stood there, smiling.

Chapter XX

I was taken to another room, kicking and screaming wildly. They carried me up a long flight of stairs and then down a narrow hallway. And at last I was alone.

A lock clicked. The voices grew faint. It was some time before I stirred from the small cot on which they had thrown me. The room was dark. My eyes traveled slowly up to the solitary window. It was barred and so high that it was impossible to see through it without standing tiptoe on the bed.

Hours passed. My head ached, and I was thirsty. At last the head nurse came into the room and turned on a small light which I had not noticed before. She held out a glass to me.

"Here, take this," she commanded. "It will help you."

With an effort I half arose from the cot.

"What is it?"

"Something to quench your thirst. You'll feel better."

The drink was cooling, and I looked up into the nurse's face eager to show my gratitude. But what I saw there stopped me.

The woman's professional air had vanished.

"Your little ruse—to see the Perkins woman worked like a charm, but you were wrong about the doctor and Miss Evangeline. I am the one going to South America with Emile.

With this she left me. My mind was working rapidly. So that's the way it is, I told myself. Evangeline wanted to rid herself of Emile's medical services. Suddenly I blinked. I was conscious of that. Then slowly my eyelids grew heavy. I brought my head up abruptly. The drink that had quenched my thirst had contained a drug. Desperately I tried to hold onto my senses. My sight was dimming. My muscles lacked co-ordination. But through my blurred thinking one point stood out. Evangeline was a devil, a devil . . . a woman scorned . . . a woman scorned. . . .

I remembered that night I had returned from my first appointment with Mrs. Wilsey and had overheard the heated conversation between Evangeline and the doctor.

"The descent has always been in the direct line," Evangeline had said. "And so it must continue to be, through me, the eldest daughter!"

And now I knew the madness that made her believe she could carry her determination through. And I knew, too, that should Evangeline ever realize that she would never get Philip, she would get rid of him. Perhaps Evangeline had already come to this realization.

It was imperative that I should warn Philip. But how could I do that? I looked hopelessly about me. The drug was working in me. I could feel it paralyzing my body, clouding my brain. All at once I could see no more. My head grew heavy. Everything was dark . . . very dark . . .

Later Jeggy Williams told me that after I had left him at the entrance to the sanitarium, he had waited patiently in the car for quite some time.

"Then I got to wondering," he said, "why Mrs. Wilsey hadn't shown up to keep the appointment."

After a time a large black sedan pulled into the drive and stopped.

"I saw it was Doc Rudlow's," Jeggy explained, "and there was Miss Evangeline sitting next to him.

The pair hurried into the building.

"I was thanking my lucky star," Jeggy said, "that they had passed me by when Miss Evangeline gives a quick backward glance in my direction. Then she says, 'You may go back to town, no need to wait for Miss Hunter. I'll see that she gets home.'

"I didn't like the looks of things," Jeggy went on to explain, "but finally I went back to town. That same evening I happened to run into Mrs. Wilsey at the drugstore."

" 'How was it you didn't meet Miss Hunter this afternoon, as you planned to, Mrs. Wilsey?' I said stopping her.

"She was some put out! 'Why,' she said, 'someone at the school phoned and said that the meeting was off. And me all set to visit my dear Aunt Evelyn!' "

Jeggy was a little worried. I was in some sort of trouble. As soon as Mrs. Wilsey went out of the store, he stepped quickly into the phone booth and called the Hall.

"Is Miss Hunter there?" he asked.

There was a long pause before an unknown voice replied, "Why no, she isn't. Miss Hunter left late this morning. She was unexpectedly called home."

Jeggy almost swallowed his tobacco cud.

"Called home, you say?"

But there was only a sharp click on the other end of the line.

Jeggy was thoroughly aroused. If I were in any danger . . . He bolted into the street. He realized now that I must still be at the sanitarium. Was I being kept there or did I want to stay? He had to find out.

Jeggy's brain was working fast. Time was important. Each minute counted. He returned to the phone booth in the drugstore. The plan was a simple one. Picking up the receiver, he called Doctor Rudlow's sanitarium.

"Hello," he raised his voice excitedly. "Hello! Hurry! Where is Doctor Rudlow?"

"The doctor is not in. Who is calling?"

"Never mind." Jeggy replied crisply. "This is an emergency. There has been an automobile accident. A man is hurt. We must get him to a hospital at once!"

"But the doctor is not here. I don't know when he will return, and there is no ambulance!"

"A passer-by is bringing the victim."

"Very well," she said at last. "Everything will be ready."

Jeggy hung up then, or almost hung up. He clicked the holder for the receiver, then delicately put the earphone on the small ledge used for writing messages in the booth.

Next, quickly as his ancient car would take him, he drove to the institution.

The doorman fortunately was nowhere in sight. Jeggy pressed a button over which was written, "Night bell," and almost immediately the door swung open. It was the head nurse herself. Jeggy pushed a big foot into the doorway.

"The accident case," Jeggy cried. "Quick! A stretcher—"

The head nurse was taken momentarily off guard. She turned her back on the newcomer and in that instant Jeggy had control of the situation. He trust a finger into the woman's back.

"Keep still," he warned, "and everything will be all right." Then, "Where is Doctor Rudlow?"

"He's not here," the woman stammered. "That's the truth!"

"Where is Miss Hunter? I know she's here."

Jeggy pressed his finger deeper into the starched back.

"Quick! Before the police arrive. They've been told everything."

Jeggy stuck his hand down into his coat pocket, still keeping his finger outstretched. It was a good imitation of the real thing. He pushed his captive around and flashed his deputy sheriff's badge.

"Talk fast!"

She took Jeggy then to the room in which I was being held. The effects of the drug had worn off somewhat, but I hardly knew what was happening. I realized, however, that we were all getting out of that place. Evelyn, Jeggy and I.

"Now I'm taking you both back to the village," Jeggy said. "You can stay the rest of the night with Mrs. Wilsey."

"No—not yet," I replied. "I must get to the school."

Then I told my companion enough of the story to obtain his co-operation. He looked at me in admiration.

"You're a brave one, Miss Hunter." And then, eagerly, he added, "I was afraid all the fun was over."

"We must be quick. Let's go!"

Soon we were tearing up the long hill toward the gates of the Hall. When we reached them, I told Jeggy it would be better for me to go on alone from there.

"Take Miss Perkins to Mrs. Wilsey," I urged. I had to get to Philip and warn him of his danger. I could do this better alone, admit myself secretly into the Hall, go quietly to Philip's room.

"I'll come back as soon as I leave Miss Perkins there," Jeggy said.

"All right! Wait for me at the gate."

I started the climb toward the Hall.

Chapter XXI

THE back door door was locked. However, there was still another way of avoiding the front of the house—the entrance near the chapel. Hopefully I circled the building.

A faint light seeping through the window blinds of the library attracted my attention. Who other than Philip would be working there at this late hour! Without further consideration I admitted myself through the front door. But as I moved toward the library I was on my guard once more, for it was not Philip's voice which came through the half-open door, but Evangeline's. If she is lying to Philip, I thought grimly. Evangeline Meredith is due to receive a rather unpleasant surprise.

I tiptoed across the Great Hall. Evangeline's voice was urgent. I could see her standing beside the library table, her body taut and menacing. The person whom she was adressing remained out of sight, but in a moment I recognized Helena's voice. I drew back to avoid discovery and was about to move away when Mrs. Hawkins came from the center passage. Quickly I ducked behind a heavy black cabinet.

Mrs. Hawkins, preoccupied, walked to the front door, opened it wide, and stood there staring into the night. My attention returned at once to the occupants of the library.

"Where is he?" Evangeline asked. "You have been here all evening. You ought to know."

"I don't go prying into the affairs of others. He was here for dinner, and then he left immediately afterward."

Evangeline paced up and down the room.

"You are excited, Evangeline. What has happened? Why have you sent for me?"

"I thought it might interest you to know that Nancy Hunter is in the Rudlow Sanitarium."

"Did she prove difficult?"

Evangeline snorted, "I allow no one to get the better of me. After tomorrow all of them will be safely out of the way. Just another few hours, and then—"

"It was clever of you to think of sending Rudlow to South America."

"We have to be clever in our position."

Evangeline's inclusion of her sister seemed a deliberate attempt to win Helena over by flattery.

"You always claimed to be the smarter one. I hope from now on we can share things as true sisters should. And now may I go? I am very tired."

"One moment. There is something else." Carefully, "Nancy Hunter knows that Eleanor was murdered."

"How does she know?"

There was terror in the younger woman's voice. "How did she find out?"

"They all know now."

"But I thought you said the danger was past. Suppose there are questions asked, what are we going to say?"

Evangeline moved back to the table.

"That is why I sent for you. By way of precaution I want you to sign these papers."

"Sign papers! What for? Let me read them through."

"Those papers appoint me your guardian."

"My guardian. My guardian! So that's it. You are very ingenious, Evangeline, but I won't be browbeaten any longer."

"Hush, you fool. Do you want to rouse everyone?"

"I don't care who hears me! You'll never have Philip, never! You're too old!" She began to laugh and cry hysterically, obviously breaking under the strain. "No man has ever desired you in spite of your good looks. What makes you think that Philip is the exception?"

Evangeline was suddenly very calm.

"I am destined to carry on our heritage. In me lives the spirit of our great-grandfather, and it will survive through my issue alone. I have kept the estate intact to that end. No outsider has a share now. Now, come, we are wasting time, sign these papers. If the truth should ever come out a plea of insanity might be your sole defense."

There was a long pause. My body felt cramped and uncomfortable. But I dared not stir now, for Mrs. Hawkins had left her post at the entrance, and seating herself on a chair diagonally opposite me, she took some knitting from a bag.

"No, no, I'll tell Philip the truth. I'll tell him exactly what you are, and about his mother—and Nancy Hunter—"

"Have you forgotten, Helena, that in the presence of our lawyer you requested that she be committed to an institution? In the eyes of the world, you and Emile alone are responsible for her detention. You played right into my hands. Philip knows how jealous you have always been of anyone who ever looked at him. How many times we were amused by your lack of subtlety. I knew what I was doing when I told you Eleanor and Philip had been reconciled. Your actions will not come as a complete surprise. If you persist in rejecting my proposal you must take the consequences—murderess!"

The telephone jangled stridently in Evangeline's office. Mrs. Hawkins hastened to answer the call.

Almost at once she ran to the library.

"Miss Evangeline, Miss Evangeline, Nancy Hunter's escaped!"

"Oh, God!" Helena screamed. "She'll come back here. I'm trapped! I'm trapped!"

"Be still," Evangeline said sharply. "Be still, Helena. Let Hawkins finish what she has to say."

"Doctor Rudlow was just on the phone. He thinks the police are on their way here now. What are we going to do?"

"The police! They'll put me in prison. Oh, Eva, help me!"

"You can help yourself by signing these papers. They will offer you protection."

There was a moment of silence broken only by the sharp scratching of the pen.

"I'm afraid," Helena moaned, "I don't want to die."

"I think it might be better for all of us if the police were not to find you here when they arrive. You must go down to the vaults. Then take the subterranean passage to the laboratory."

"No! Not the passage. Something might happen to me there in the dark. It's so slippery."

"Nonsense. There's a flashlight in this drawer. You can't lose your way. The Lord knows, we were down there enough when we were children."

"You weren't, Evangeline. You always made the rest of us go down and then you ran away with the light. What will I do when I reach the laboratory, anyway? I don't like your idea at all. I'm not going."

"Oh—yes—you are."

Helena was pushed out of the room and led down the hall by Evangeline and Mrs. Hawkins.

"Stay in the stone house until you see the police car pass," Evangeline instructed rapidly. "Then hurry to the gate. Meanwhile I'll telephone Emile to have a car meet you on that little trail off the road. In a few hours you can sail with him."

By this time they were out of sight and I cautiously stole down the passageway.

The entrance to the mausoleum was back near the kitchen. I moved along, carefully hugging the wall. The creaking of rusty hinges sounded weirdly in the stillness. It was the door to the tomb. I waited for what seemed like hours.

A single, terror-stricken cry rent the air. Evangeline must have shoved her sister down those long, iron steps. Then the grating sound was repeated. A long silence. Then voices—coming nearer.

A classroom yawned behind me, and I slipped quickly into its protective darkness as Evangeline and Mrs. Hawkins came down the passage.

"Make haste!" Evangeline was saying. "Run down and block the trap door in the laboratory. She must never get out, or we're lost."

Mrs. Hawkins hurried away. Evangeline paused in the hallway. Then she took a step and impatiently tugged at the pull bell. In a few minutes Maggie appeared in a kimono, rubbing sleepily at her eyes.

"Get dressed at once," Evangeline commanded. "I want you to search the building for Miss Hunter. Bring her to me when you find her. All the doors are locked but she has a key to the front entrance. And, wait, you had better lock Mary in her room."

As soon as Maggie was out of sight, Evangeline hurried to her office. Now I was in great danger. I could no longer remain in the schoolroom. I had to reach Philip before the servant started the search. Darkness shrouded me as I groped my way up the back stairs.

A dim light burned in the second-floor corridor. I sped to Philip's room. The door was open. No one was there! Then panic gripped me. Like Helena, I began to feel trapped.

I decided to risk getting out at the front of the building. I moved toward the landing, anxious eyes peering over the balustrade. Evangeline's office door opened and she came out. A tiny pistol glittered in her hand.

Suddenly a door slammed. There were footsteps in the corridor. Someone was running toward the front of the house. Evangeline wheeled, her fingers closing tightly on the metal.

It was Mrs. Hawkins. She was breathless.

"Mr. James," she panted, "is coming up the driveway."

The front door opened, and Evangeline's right hand slipped into the pocket of her dress. After that one brief gesture no one looking at the woman would have known that she was under a strain.

"Philip," she began, "I've been waiting for you—"

"Where's Nancy?"

"Nancy? Why, don't you know that she was called home?"

"That's a lie, Evangeline. Jeggy Williams told me Nancy came here this evening."

Evangeline's eyes fixed on Mrs. Hawkins. I almost saw the message that was being telegraphed in that brief glance. Then Mrs. Hawkins disappeared down the center passage.

"Of course, Philip, if you prefer someone else's word to mine—"

"If you've done anything to harm her, by God I'll—"

But the rest of his words were lost in an ear-splitting blast. Meredith Hall shuddered on its foundations. Philip dashed to the door.

"My God. It's the laboratory. There's been an explosion."

He turned and caught the queer expression on Evangeline's face, madness mingled with triumph. Misunderstanding, he cried out, "Nancy is there—"

And then he was out of the building before I could call out to tell him I was still safe.

Hawkins rushed into the hall.

"It must be Miss Helena. She'll be blown to bits. I heard a car coming—I only had time to lock the outer door."

Pandemonium broke loose in the dormitories. Students started pouring down the stairs, flocking to windows and doorways. Faculty and servants scattered to the different exits.

Evangeline's deep voice could be heard above the din.

"Quiet, everyone. There is no cause for alarm. Return to your rooms, all of you!"

I took advantage of the temporary confusion, and pressed forward anxiously through the surging crowd, seeking to flee while there was yet a chance.

But Evangeline moved rapidly through the throng. Again I caught the gleam of steel in her hand. Her eyes traveled past me, and I turned involuntarily. Hawkins was bearing down on me from the landing.

Evangeline came closer.

"Stop her, Hawkins," she cried as I dashed across the hall.

I darted wildly through the doorway. With Evangeline close on my heels I raced toward the blazing laboratory. I was temporarily shielded by the heavy thicket. The smoke-filled air choked me as I drove myself forward. She was not swifter than I, but she was stronger and gained upon me as my strength failed.

I reached the clearing. Only two hundred feet to Philip and safety. There was another explosion, followed by a whirling hell of flame.

Someone shouted, "It's no use."

And then Philip's voice, "We mustn't stop, there's someone inside."

That was all I needed to hear. I ran across the clearing, wildly shrieking his name. A stinging pain stabbed my shoulder.

Philip saw me then, and he recognized Evangeline, too—a tall, menacing figure with the gun still clutched in her hand.

She would have killed us both had it not been for the crowd moving away from the wall of flame where the roundhouse had stood. Philip held me close in his arms. I heard him whisper, "Thank God, you're safe," and then I fainted.

When I opened my eyes, I was in a strange room. I sat up with a start.

"You're all right, dear," Philip whispered. "This is Mrs. Wilsey's house. Just lie back and rest."

He came and sat at my bedside while he told he everything that had happened. Rudlow had been caught while trying to escape. Helena's remains had been dug out of the charred ruins.

Fearfully I inquired about Evangeline.

She had vanished. The grounds and the crypt were searched, but she was nowhere to be found.

Although the fire left the main building untouched, the school was closed. Cornelia Fiske, George Mundin, Henrietta Valentine, Mrs. Hawkins and Geoffery Carter all scattered, each to seek his destiny far from Meredith Hall, and soon legends grew out of Evangeline Meredith's strange disappearance. Villagers in the vicinity of the Hall were said to have heard the organ playing on moonlit nights, wafting its frenzied music through the silent gloom.

Years later, when there was talk of demolishing the old building, I learned what had become of Evangeline. Workmen exploring the lower regions came upon the family mausoleum. In Silas Meredith's vault they found a corpse whose brown garments crumbled into dust when they were disturbed.

THE END